3

There Were Three of Us in the Marriage (or so I thought . . .)

In the stylish and crumb-free kitchen of the Vauxhall apartment of her very good friend, Adelaide Charles, Janet Parnell fiddled nervously with the collar of her blouse. Did Adelaide know? Was that why she had called her, requesting she come to visit 'this morning, at your earliest convenience'?

Adelaide, symmetrical as ever, dressed in her simple, perfect pastels, sat down in the chair opposite Janet, pushed a tin of biscuits across the table and smiled. 'Would you like a biscuit? I've got these delightful, simply delightful ginger creams from a local baker. I do like to support local small businesses, don't you? And I do so like that blouse you're wearing. So many colours! So daring! You must tell me where you got it from.' Adelaide adjusted her Alice band. 'Oh, and, now before I forget, how long have you been having an affair with my husband?'

Janet dropped the simply delightful ginger cream biscuit, and it fell into her cup of Earl Grey, causing tea to splash onto the marble table-top. 'Oh.'

'Yes,' said Adelaide, still smiling. 'Oh, indeed.'

Janet began to gabble as she used her sleeve to try and mop up the splashes of tea. It wasn't just that Adelaide was her good friend, but it was an unspoken truth that Adelaide Charles was the leader of their social group. One word from Adelaide Charles and there'd be no more charming afternoon teas, no more charity functions, no more candlelit suppers. 'Please, Adelaide, I'm so sorry, I'm so so sorry, it just happened. You know I've been depressed since Sanjay left me, and Oliver, dear Oliver, he was so kind to me.'

Adelaide nodded. 'Oliver is very kind, isn't he? Very generous.' She toyed with her necklace.

The necklace, like Adelaide's clothes and hair and make-up, was simple, understated and not at all ostentatious. Janet knew that it cost a small fortune to look that inexpensive. She started to cry.

Adelaide sighed. 'Oh, Janet, do stop blubbing. You're not the only one, you know.'

Janet flinched. Somehow Adelaide's calm, unbothered reaction seemed really rather cruel. It was as if none of it really mattered. 'I'm not the only what?'

Adelaide turned towards the door and called out. 'You can come in now.'

The door opened and the most beautiful man Janet had ever seen strutted into the kitchen. He was tall and blond, well-built, so so handsome. He wore tight jeans and a checked shirt. And he was smirking.

'Janet, darling, don't stare.' Adelaide was also smirking. 'This is Danny. Danny works on that farm, you know. The one next to the park that working-class children visit so they can see what geese and llamas look like.'

'Erm, hello,' said Janet, feeling her cheeks blush. 'Erm, well, it's jolly nice to meet you. I think.'

Adelaide stood up, walked over to Danny, linked arms with him and escorted him back towards Janet. Janet tried to take a sip of her Earl Grey to calm her nerves and ended up with a mouthful of ginger cream biscuit sludge. She tried to swallow it down, listening as Adelaide held court.

'This is Danny. Oh, don't speak, Danny, you're far too pretty to try and do words. Oliver has been having an affair with Danny since Christmas, would you believe.'

Janet was stunned and cried out. 'But he's a man!'

Adelaide chuckled. 'You are sweet. Now, the thing is, Oliver doesn't know that I know about Danny. Which is good because, at Christmas, I was the one who paid Danny to seduce my husband.'

Janet's mind was reeling. 'I don't understand,' she said.

'It's quite simple. Danny will give me evidence of his affair with my husband. I can then divorce my husband and, because he had the affair, I'll get everything. I'll be independently wealthy, imagine that!'

Janet nodded, realising that she wasn't actually that surprised by Adelaide's deception. She had always been clever. Janet quickly did what Janet always did: she offered to support Adelaide in order to stay by her side and bask in her social standing.

'I could get evidence as well!' she yelped. 'Let me help you, Adelaide!'

Adelaide smiled. 'Oh, my dear, my darling Janet, you already have helped me. You see, Danny here – no, petal, sweet Danny, don't talk – Danny here has obtained evidence of my husband's affair with you.'

'Oh,' said Janet.

'Oh, indeed,' said Adelaide. 'So, there's been a slight change of plan. What is going to happen is that Oliver is going to be informed that you plan to release this damning evidence so he's going to do something very, very naughty indeed. He's going to kill you.'

Janet blinked slowly then burst out laughing. 'But, what? He wouldn't do that! What?'

'Well, of course he wouldn't.' Adelaide nodded. 'You know that. I know that. Even Danny, who went to a comprehensive school, knows that.'

There was a long pause as Janet tried to work out what Adelaide was saying. She looked up at her friend, who smiled at her then nodded down at the cup of Earl Grey. Janet looked down at the cup and then back up at Adelaide. Adelaide nodded down at the cup. Janet looked down at the cup and then back up at Adelaide, still very confused.

Adelaide sighed. 'Did you enjoy your tea, dear?'

And finally Janet understood. Just as she realised she was having trouble breathing.

'This way, I won't need a divorce.' Adelaide sat down next to her and held Janet's hand. 'Oliver will go to prison for killing you and I'll be free. And rich.'

Janet realised, very quickly, that there was nothing she could do. She was struggling to breathe, but, despite everything, she couldn't help but look up at Danny again. He really was devastatingly handsome. Like Brad Pitt's better-looking brother.

As darkness started to fill her vision, Janet received one final surprise. The kitchen door opened, and the hulking form of Oliver Charles slithered into the room.

'Oh, you're all here,' he said. 'How marvellous!'

Adelaide turned to him with a triumphant sneer. 'Yes! And you're going to pay for everything you've done.'

Oliver started to laugh. 'Oh, my beautiful wife, you're so ... human. All of this, all of everything you've done here, paying Danny, poisoning Janet, all of it and for what?'

'You knew?' whispered Adelaide.

Janet, realising she could no longer move because her whole body was shutting down, was nevertheless thrilled to see the shock on Adelaide's face.

Oliver laughed and laughed as he closed the kitchen door and locked it. 'The thing is, I've got to go into town for some business with the family,' he said. 'You, you and you, you've all been so much fun. So, I was going to let you live ...'

Adelaide moved behind Danny, who raised his fists up at Oliver. So gallant, thought Janet, as her eyes started to glaze over.

Oliver Charles smiled and, as he towered over his wife and his lover, he did something that Janet couldn't really comprehend. There was something on his forehead. A brilliant light. Obviously, her brain was shutting down because of the poison but, even so, it just didn't make sense.

But Janet Parnell smiled. Because she knew for sure, somehow, that Adelaide Charles and the handsome Danny were going to die as well. As she died, she heard the roar of something flying over the house. She would never know what it was.

4

Clock This!

'What appears to be a flying object of unknown origin is currently flying over the city of London ...'

Newsreaders across the world interrupted scheduled broadcasting with the biggest news of the century. And the world watched live!

PC Tristan White had finally reached the front of the queue at Jim's Café. He was just about to order when someone shouted for Jim to turn on the small black-and-white television set sitting on the shelf next to the ketchup bottles. PC White, seeing the news, realised he would be skipping his bacon butty today.

Molly Steer was in the middle of doing her crossword. She already had the telly on in the background for company. She carefully put down her pencil and newspaper as she watched the spaceship fly over London. 'Well, that can't be good,' she muttered to Denis's empty chair.

Jackie Tyler was sitting alone in the dark with a cup of sweet tea. She didn't have the television on, and she was so preoccupied with wondering where her daughter had been for the last year that she didn't even notice the spaceship roaring over the Powell Estate.

Mickey Smith, still unaware that his girlfriend had returned to Earth, was sitting in his flat, updating his website. He had found some grainy footage of the man he believed to be the Doctor doing the Charleston on the roof of Buckingham Palace and was wondering if he could use it to prove that aliens existed when the spaceship flew so low over his top-floor flat that every window shattered. 'Now they'll have to believe me!' he told the photo of Rose that sat next to his computer.

At Number 10 Downing Street, the Prime Minister of the United Kingdom was having peppermint tea and marmalade on toast with the Queen of England when, through the window, he saw the spaceship flying over London. Stunned, he swore – and then quickly apologised to the Queen for his language. He'd been so distracted by the spaceship that he hadn't heard the extremely naughty word the Queen herself had used.

In a secluded sunny corner of the Powell Estate, a sleepy fox, not watching the television, dreamed about chips ...

And the Doctor and Rose were running. The Doctor had suggested trying to get a bus into the city centre, but Rose knew that, even without the spaceship, there'd be traffic jams as commuters would already be heading to work. Their best bet, she told him, would be the Tube. It would be packed, but it would be running. As they ran towards Kennington station, Rose suddenly stopped and turned to stare at a shop window. It was a branch of Magpie Electricals and in the window, on sale, were a number of television sets. Each was showing the breaking news. The Doctor, realising she had stopped, ran back and joined her.

They watched as the spaceship seemed to speed up as it arced towards Big Ben. Rose held her breath and the Doctor quickly took her hand as they watched. The spaceship crashed noisily into the most famous clock in the world, grinding through the walls of St Stephen's Tower and sending the arms of the clock hurtling down into the River Thames like a pair of harpoons, The spaceship smashed into the bell of the clock, causing it to clang discordantly, before both bell and spaceship spiralled down and joined the rest of the debris in the river. For a second, everything seemed to be silent. The world watched on television as the city of London tried to comprehend the magnitude of what had just happened. And then the sirens and the screaming started ...

The Doctor took Rose's hand as she stared in silence. 'I can't believe I'm here to see this,' he said. 'This is fantastic.'

Rose shivered, despite the morning sun. 'Did you know this was going to happen?'

'Nope.'

'Do you recognise the ship?'

'Nope.'

'Do you know why it crashed?'

'Nope.'

His casual northern tone made Rose momentarily forget the images she had just seen, and she smirked. 'Oh, I'm so glad I've got you.'

Clearly not sensing her sarcasm, the Doctor turned to her with a big grin. 'I bet you are. This is what I travel for, Rose. To see history happening right in front of us.'

'Well, let's go and see it,' she replied. But as she turned towards the Underground station, she saw a man in a hi-vis jacket shutting the metal gates. The centre of London was already being put into lockdown. The adventure was happening without them.

Jackie Tyler was staring down into her cold cup of tea when she realised she could hear something ringing. Someone was ringing the doorbell. Still in a state of shock, she stood, walked through the hallway and opened the front door. Standing in front of her were her neighbours Ru and Bau from number 136. Ru was supporting her husband, who seemed to be having difficulty standing.

'What is it, what's wrong?' asked Jackie.

'The spaceship!' exclaimed Ru. 'Bau nearly had a heart attack!'

'The what?' Jackie had no idea what Ru was talking about but quickly realised that Bau looked to be in a bad way. She ushered them into the flat, her fearful worries about Rose vanishing as she took control of this new situation. 'His heart? Right, you two go sit down. Apple cider vinegar, that's what my nan used to swear by.'

As Ru took Bau into the living room, she called back to Jackie. 'Why don't you have the television on?'

Jackie, confused, was about to close the front door when suddenly Mrs Boufakis from number 24 appeared in the doorway like a timid hedgehog. 'I'm so sorry, dear, it's just I'm on my own and obviously I'm a little nervous, and I thought who's good in a crisis, well, it's Jackie Tyler, isn't it. Would you mind if I came in?'

Without waiting for permission, Mrs Boufakis inched past Jackie and joined Ru and Bau in the living room.

'What crisis?' asked Jackie as she closed the door and went to join them. 'What's this crisis you're all on about?'

'The spaceship!' said Mrs Boufakis, Ru and Bau in unison as they tried to work out how to switch on the television.

Rose and the Doctor ran through the deserted courtyard of the Powell Estate.

'Everyone's stayed in, watching the telly,' explained Rose. She looked over at the TARDIS. 'Wait, we could get into town using the TARDIS!'

'They've already got one spaceship in the middle of London. I don't want to shove another one on top.'

'Yeah, but yours looks like a big blue box. No one's going to notice.'

'You'd be surprised.' The Doctor started striding towards the stairwell, calling back to Rose.

'Emergency like this, there'll be all kinds of people watching. Trust me, the TARDIS stays where it is.'

Rose thought about what he had meant. People watching out for him? If the Doctor was nine hundred years old, did he have other friends on Earth? Or even enemies?

Cardiff, Wales. A man, his face hidden in the shadows, talks to a young woman.

'Owen's sick, so you'll have to go.' His voice sounds American, but she suspects he's not from America.

She's confused. 'I'm not a medic, surely the army won't let me in?'

The man hands her some documents. 'Signed by the Queen herself. You get access to whatever crashed that spaceship and you wait.'

'And if he's there?'

'This is the first mass public sighting of a UFO,' the man replies. 'He'll be there.'

She tries to stop her hand shaking. 'I'm scared, Jack.'

He reaches out and takes her hand and she realises he has given her a small pistol. 'You'll need this.' Then he disappears back into the shadows.

The young woman, Toshiko Sato, steps out into the Cardiff sunshine and hails a taxi. She asks the driver to take her to the heliport just outside of the city. She takes a deep breath as she settles back into the car seat. Today is the day that she will meet the Doctor.

'We've got sausage rolls on the bottom shelf, mini chicken kiev things on the middle shelf and something that smells like beans on the top shelf. Take the sausage rolls out first, then move the kievs down otherwise they'll leak.' Jackie Tyler handed a pair of oven gloves to Molly Steer and picked up a tray of drinks. She pushed through the Latifs from number 12 and popped the tray down on the living room table. 'Right, these are Spritz but I don't have any prosecco so it's just wine.'

'You're a star, Jackie Tyler,' called out Brian, one of the gays from number 67. He had his arm around Brainy Betty, who was telling anyone who would listen her theories about the UFO.

'Well, it's a big day, isn't it! First, my Rose comes home and then a spaceship hits Big Ben!' Jackie looked over at Rose and the Doctor, who were both sitting cross-legged watching the television. 'Oh, and that Billy Croot asked me out. Not that madam cares.'

'You've broken your mother's heart,' Ru called out at Rose, as she nibbled a sandwich. Her husband,

Bau, was already asleep, snoring on the sofa next to her. Rose ignored her, her eyes fixed on the news as army divers started to enter the Thames to look for the spaceship.

'Ooh, that reporter's dishy,' shouted out Jackie, cackling. 'Right, cola for the kiddies!' A gaggle of children drawing spaceships on the wall in the hallway cheered.

Tom Hitchinson, blissfully unaware that Jackie Tyler thought he was dishy, had started the day getting ready for a trip to Hull to film a report about the city's rich fishing history. He had only been working at BBC News for three weeks and was still very much being given the smaller human interest stories to report on. He and his cameraman, Stu, had been just about to board the train at Kings Cross station when the spaceship had roared across the sky above them. Before Tom could even ask, 'Was that actually a spaceship roaring across the sky above us?', Stu had his camera out from its case, pointing at the sky, and was running towards the action. Tom, quickly realising that this would be the scoop of the century, had followed. Now, standing on Westminster Bridge, reporting to the world, Tom was suddenly very aware of how freaked out he was. He'd wanted to tell the big stories. He'd wanted to report on the juicy stuff. But he was suddenly incredibly apprehensive about just how close to the action he was. What if there were actual aliens in the spaceship? What if something came out and started to attack people? What if it wanted to eat people? He watched as the red light flashed on top of the camera, and he gazed out at millions of viewers across the world, trying not to show any fear.

'I'm Tom Hitchinson, reporting live for BBC News,' he announced. 'I'm standing on Westminster Bridge, as the army are sending down divers into the wreck of the spaceship. No one knows what they're going to find.'

In New York, Trinity Wells was having her hair fixed as she quickly sat down behind the news desk. It was still early and Americans on the East Coast were only just waking up to the news. She shooed away the make-up and hair gals and forced herself to stop grinning. This was major news, the biggest news of the century. People would look back on the coverage of these incredible events and they would remember Trinity Wells.

She fixed a concerned look on her face as she turned to the cameras and dramatically announced,

'I'm Trinity Wells and you're watching AMNN on the day that the world discovered that we are not alone.'

As she reported on the events in London, adding some extra speculation about other cities that might be attacked, Trinity Wells pictured the awards she'd receive in the future. Perhaps, one day, she'd even have her own show?

'Of course, Paris in France also has a river, so could the next spaceship land there?' she asked, adding an assurance to the audience that she didn't want to speculate on what might happen.

More neighbours had arrived at Jackie's flat, and she was handing out paper plates and telling people to help themselves as she only had two hands. The Doctor and Rose stared at the television as Tom Hitchinson continued his live report.

'And I can confirm,' he announced gravely, 'that the divers have found a body in the spaceship.'

Behind the Doctor and Rose, Beryl Thompson, hovering with a quiche, heard this and gasped. 'They've found a body! They've found a body!' She collapsed into a chair. 'Aliens!'

As everyone in the room started to speculate about what the aliens might look like, Rose turned away from the screen to look at the Doctor. 'Should we be scared?'

He turned to face her and smiled. She might have only known him for a few days, but she knew when his smile wasn't real. She knew he was worried. Really worried.

Suddenly, the front door burst open and Sandra and Jason from number 44 came crashing in, wearing party hats and carrying a bottle in each hand. Everyone cheered. Except for Rose and the Doctor.

At 10 Downing Street, his tea and toast with the Queen having been prematurely brought to an end, the Prime Minister was getting an update on the situation from one of his junior aides.

'What have you got for me, Indra?' he asked, leaning back on his desk. He always made a point of using someone's first name to show that he was a kind and caring Prime Minister.

Indra Ganesh handed over the latest report. 'They're taking the body to Albion Hospital, sir. But...'

'But what?'

'Here's a photo, sir, of, well... of the alien, sir.'

The Prime Minister looked at the photograph. 'But that's...'

'Yes, sir.'

'Well, you'd better leave it with me, Indra. Thank you.'

Indra turned and left the room, closing the door behind him.

The Prime Minister walked round his desk and slumped into his chair. It just didn't make sense. As he stared at the photograph, he really started to regret having recently given up caffeine. He suspected this was going to be the longest day of his career and he was dying for a strong black coffee. He took a deep breath then began to work out a plan of action. The first thing he would do would be to call his wife and make sure she and the kids left London immediately. He'd seen the film *Independence Day* and he knew that the aliens always went after the cities first.

There was a knock at the door.

'Come in,' he called out, as he started writing out his to-do list. 'Number one, call wifey,' he muttered. 'Number two, read the Emergency Protocols ...'

The door opened. 'Hello, Prime Minister,' said a voice. 'I'm so glad to have caught you on your own.'

The Prime Minister of the United Kingdom looked up from his list as the owner of the voice started to giggle ...

5

A New Prime Minister

General Ronald Theodore Asquith had never seen an alien before. As Chief of the Defence Staff, he was the head of the British Armed Forces and the highest-ranking military adviser to the Prime Minister. He'd seen terrible things while serving in the Navy during the Falklands war and had more recently read reports from Iraq that had made him feel physically sick. He'd seen so much of the world, including islands that weren't on maps and a waterfall in Chile that flowed upwards, defying gravity. He'd even been to the moon recently as plans to build a base there had firmed up.

But General Ronald Asquith had never seen an alien in the flesh.

Obviously, he knew the truth about the Nestene Consciousness's attack a year before but there had been nothing left of that creature after its destruction at the hands of the Doctor. At least, that was the official story. He had always secretly suspected that there may have been some remains but that Yvonne and her yuppie boys and girls at Torchwood had got there first.

A year before, General Asquith had helped formulate the gas leak story to help cover up the truth of the Nestene attack. Today, as he stepped into the infirmary, though, he was still taking in the gravity of this new situation. The whole world had seen the spaceship crash into Big Ben. The whole world was watching what was happening on television. Could they even try to cover this up?

He stopped and looked over at the single bed that stood in the middle of the room. The room was cold, blue, a single white light shining down onto the white sheet that covered the small shape underneath. Small, he thought. That was good. Small was less of a threat than big. Seeing the shape in front of him meant that his fears were already being pushed aside and his brain was automatically doing what he was good at – analysing the situation and working out a response.

Everything was going to be hunky-dory.

'Sir?' A voice behind him made him jump and, to his shame, he let out a tiny squeal. He turned to see a very young, very pretty doctor.

'Crikey,' he said then, regaining his composure, he introduced himself.

The doctor gave him a professional smile. He noticed that she was holding tightly on to a handbag. 'I'm Dr Sato, sir,' she said, holding out her free hand. 'Toshiko.'

He shook her hand, and they moved over to the bed. He indicated for her to pull back the sheet. He stared down at the body. It was very much not what he'd expected an alien to look like.

'Good god. And that's real? It's not a hoax or a dummy?'

'I've X-rayed the skull,' replied Dr Sato. 'It's wired up inside like nothing I've ever seen before. No one could make this up.'

'We've got experts being flown in. Until they arrive, get that out of sight.'

He turned and marched back out into the corridor.

Toshiko Sato closed the door of the locker, sealing the alien inside. She waited for General Asquith to leave the room then she slumped down into a chair. She felt as if she had been holding her breath for the last hour. She'd been worried about the Government working out that she wasn't from the army or the army working out that she wasn't from the

Government or anyone working out that she wasn't really a doctor. She reached under the chair and picked up her handbag. She looked at the small pistol inside the bag and shuddered. She waited for the Doctor.

In the corridor, General Asquith took out his phone and allowed himself to relax slightly. He knew that Frost's team were flying over from Geneva, and he was pretty certain he'd kept Yvonne and Torchwood away from the situation. This was good, things were going well. He pressed the key on his phone that would take him directly to the Prime Minister's hotline. As he waited for the Prime Minister to answer, he started to work out some possible cover-up explanations. An advertising campaign for a new Hollywood movie? A meteorite? Could they perhaps even frame a foreign power – claim that it hadn't been a spaceship but some kind of military attack vehicle? This was good. A war was always good for the country's finances. General Asquith had options to present to the Prime Minister.

But the Prime Minister wasn't answering his phone.

Indra Ganesh stared at the Prime Minister's phone as it rang.

He was in front of the Prime Minister's desk. The office was like the *Mary Celeste*. His boss had clearly been writing a to-do list and had got as far as '2) Read the Emergency Protocols'. There was a cup of cold peppermint tea and a suit jacket was on the back of the chair. Indra had already searched all over Downing Street for the Prime Minister but he seemed to have vanished.

He stared at the ringing telephone. It was the Prime Minister's personal hotline and it was forbidden for anyone else to answer it. Indra was starting to panic. A spaceship had crashed into Big Ben! The Prime Minister was missing!

'Read the Emergency Protocols ...' That's what he would do. He scurried over to a filing cabinet and took out a small red leather box. The Emergency Protocols explained what actions should be taken in the event of an alien incursion. As the telephone finally stopped ringing, Indra started to read ... 'The Prime Minister should be kept informed of everything at all times ...' Yes, but there was no Prime Minister, the Prime Minister was missing. His eyes scanned down quickly, looking for what action he should take.

'What to do if the Prime Minister is unreachable ...'

Leaving the office with the protocols, Indra continued to read...

Jackie Tyler was sitting on the side of her bath. She took a deep breath in. Then she breathed out. As the sounds of the party filled her flat, she wiped away the tears that had suddenly appeared, causing her to run to the bathroom before anybody could see.

'You're being very silly, Jacqueline Prentice,' she muttered to herself, remembering how her mum had used to scold her. She thought back to her childhood, that tiny little red-brick house in Streatham. Everything had been so simple back then. They'd had no money at all, but they'd survived. Nan had lived through the war. Mum had grown up with rationing. Jackie knew she came from a long line of women who coped. A long line of women who'd often had to cope with useless men.

'But you weren't always useless, Pete,' she whispered to herself. 'I wish you were here.'

The thing that nobody knew was that recently Jackie had started to accept that she might never see her daughter again. She'd hadn't told anybody, of course. If anyone had even tried to suggest to her that Rose might be dead and that maybe Jackie should move on, she'd shouted and raged at them.

But the truth was, she had started to think, deep down, that maybe Rose wasn't coming back.

That morning, Jackie had woken up and she had made herself some tea. She'd been planning on going to the police station as usual then lunch with Sarah and Bev. All three of them had said that they wouldn't be doing lunchtime wine but all three of them had known not to make afternoon plans. It would have been a nice day.

Then Rose had just appeared, standing there in the living room, and she wouldn't say where she'd been and then there was this man, this Doctor, and he wouldn't say where they'd been and then a flipping great spaceship had smashed into Big Ben and what had everyone done? 'Let's go to Jackie's. Jackie can cope. Jackie throws the best parties. Jackie won't be scared that aliens are real and that aliens are here and that they might be invading on the actual day her daughter came back. Jackie's a good laugh; Jackie's fine and can cope with everything.'

She mouthed silently at the bathroom door, 'I'm not fine! Why can't any of you see that I'm not fine?'

Then she remembered her mum's favourite song. 'Behind a Painted Smile' by The Isley Brothers. A song about hiding your tears.

Jackie stood up and looked at her reflection in the mirror. The smile painted itself on her face. Then she turned, opened the bathroom door and called out as she rejoined the party. 'Ooh, did you lot hear, Mad Maddy's got a load of dodgy phone top-up cards! Cheap at half the price!'

Indra Ganesh, standing in the entrance hallway of 10 Downing Street, looked up as the MP for Hartley Dale towered over him. He tried not to let out a nervous squeal. Growing up in the small town of Tarminster, Indra had been the only boy at his school with brown skin. He'd also been incredibly clever. He'd not been very tall or very sporty and, he had realised as he grew older, he wasn't interested in girls, not in the way he was supposed to be. Indra Ganesh had, from a very early age, realised that he was facing years of bullying unless he very quickly did something about it. So Indra had become the class joker. He would do impressions of his teachers and schoolmates. He would hide fake spiders in desk drawers. He'd even once managed to convince the school headmaster that the local education authority had called to shut the school down for the day because of woodworm. Indra had become especially popular at school after arranging for that day off for everyone. After sixth form, Indra left Tarminster to go to university in Oxford and he had never looked back. Now, as one of the Prime Minister's closest aides, Indra was happy with how his life was going. He had a career that made his mother and father proud, he could afford decent suits, he had a flat with amazing views in Canary Wharf and he had recently started seeing a systems analyst called Bob. Indra Ganesh was on top of the world.

Now, though, Indra was looking up at Joseph Green and remembering how he had felt on that very first day at school. Joseph Green was huge. He was easily a foot taller than Indra and twice as wide. Indra remembered a book he'd read as a child where a character had been described as having hands as large as hams and, right now, he finally understood what that meant. Joseph Green was standing in the doorway at 10 Downing Street and he was literally causing an eclipse.

Indra forced himself to smile politely and asked Mr Green to please follow him, please and thank you.

The MP for Hartley Dale gave a wolfish smile and followed him into the Prime Minister's office. 'Where is the Prime Minister?' he demanded, looking around the room, his voice like thunder.

Indra thought about what he had read in the Emergency Protocols. In the event of the Prime Minister being unreachable ... He looked up as the giant took a step closer to him.

'Where's the Prime Minister?' Green asked again. Indra could smell the man's breath, and he had to force himself not to gag. He turned away, took a deep breath and then turned back with a weak smile. Joseph Green was the most senior MP they could find in Westminster today, and the Emergency Protocols stated that, in the event of an alien incursion, the number one priority for the staff at Downing Street was to ensure that the country had strong and stable leadership.

'No one knows, sir. He's disappeared. I have to inform you that, with the city gridlocked and the Cabinet stranded outside London ...' Indra took a deep breath. 'I'm pretty sure that makes you acting Prime Minister with immediate effect.'

Joseph Green looked down at Indra, like a cat eyeing a mouse. He smiled.

And then Joseph Green, the acting Prime Minister of the United Kingdom, farted.

Indra looked up at Joseph Green. Joseph Green looked down at Indra. Indra quietly said he would bring through some paperwork for the new

Prime Minister to sign and quickly scurried out of the room.

Indra closed the door behind him and collapsed back against it. He'd lost the real Prime Minister, a spaceship had crashed through Big Ben and now the acting Prime Minister was demonstrating both horrifically bad breath and flatulence. He looked over towards the front door that led out onto Downing Street then closed his eyes. He could just run. He could run and keep running until he reached his flat in Canary Wharf. He could call Bob, and they could have a vegetarian Bolognese and watch the latest episode of *Spooks*. They could just hide away from everything that was happening.

But Indra knew he couldn't do any of that. He just needed a moment's peace and then he'd start dealing with the situation.

'Excuse me,' said a voice in his ear. He opened his eyes to see a middle-aged woman in a cheap peach suit hovering near him. 'Harriet Jones. MP for Flydale North.'

'I'm sorry,' he replied, heading down the corridor to return to his office. 'Can it wait?'

'But I did have an appointment at 11.15,' she said, following him.

'Yes, and a spaceship crashed in the middle of London,' Indra replied curtly. 'I think the schedule might have changed.' He entered his office and slammed the door closed behind him.

Harriet Jones, MP for Flydale North, sighed. The young man was right, of course. Today was turning out to be quite the day. On the train down, she'd been so excited to be finally meeting the Prime Minister and then, as announced over the speakers by a shocked train driver, the world had changed forever. Perhaps, she thought, she could help.

'What do we need in a time of crisis?' she muttered to herself. 'Coffee.'

As she turned to head back down the corridor, she found herself face-to-face with a large slab of a woman with very sensible hair and very sensible shoes.

'Are you looking for Mr Ganesh?' asked Harriet. 'I'm Harriet Jones, MP for Flydale North.'

The woman smiled and Harriet tried not to visibly shudder. The woman's breath stank of eggs, and she seemed to have far too many teeth.

'I'm Margaret Blaine. I'm with MI5, would you believe.' The woman with too many teeth giggled.

Rose looked around her bedroom for the first time since she'd returned home She closed the door, trying to shut out the noise of the party that was now taking place in the living room. She lay down on her bed. How often had she lain there listening to her mum and her friends drinking and laughing in the living room? Rose grinned, suddenly remembering how she used to picture them as geese.

She stopped grinning, remembering again the pain on her mum's face just a few hours before. She looked around her room, the bright pink walls and bedding, the photos on the wall and the CDs in a heap on the floor. It was all exactly as she had left it. She wondered how many times during the last year her mum had sat on this bed and cried. Rose, staring up at the ceiling, knew that at some point soon she would need to decide what she was going to do. She couldn't give up her life with the Doctor but, one day many years ago, Jackie Tyler had gone to a wedding with her husband and later that day she had returned alone. What if something happened to Rose? Would the Doctor come back here and tell her that her daughter – like her husband – was never coming home again?

There was a knock at the door.

'Come in,' Rose called out.

Jackie entered. She was smiling. 'You all right, sweetheart?'

Rose nodded. 'Mum, I wish I could tell you, you know that, right?'

Jackie shrugged.

'But I was having the best time,' continued Rose. 'Honestly, it's all good.'

Jackie shrugged. 'They're all at Downing Street now.'

'Who are?'

'I dunno,' said Jackie. 'On the telly. All the important people.'

Rose smiled. 'Not all of them. There's a very important person standing in front of me right now.'

Jackie smirked.

'Mum,' Rose continued. 'Where's Mickey?'

'Didn't you call him?'

'No, but half the estate's here. Did something happen?'

Jackie shook her head. 'Anyway, you should probably know your Doctor's gone.'

Rose's entire world lurched. She jumped to her feet. 'Gone? What do you mean gone? He wouldn't just go.'

Jackie shrugged and stepped back into the hallway. Rose belted past her and out of the front door. Outside, she looked down into the courtyard and saw the Doctor heading towards the TARDIS. She started running towards the stairs.

Surely he wasn't going to leave her?

Indra Ganesh escorted Margaret Blaine to the Prime Minister's office, trying not to visibly react to her breath. He knocked on the door and entered.

Joseph Green looked up from behind the desk. 'Hello, little man,' he said with a grin. 'And who's this?'

'Margaret Blaine,' Indra replied. 'She's with MI5.'

Margaret ignored Indra and approached Joseph. 'There's no more information, sir. I personally escorted the Prime Minister from the cabinet room to his car.'

Indra, stunned, turned to look at her. Why hadn't he been told? Where was the Prime Minister? Surely this meant that the man behind the desk now had no right to be the Prime Minister? He was about to say something when Margaret Blaine continued.

'And this is Oliver Charles, transport liaison.'

Indra gasped as he felt a huge fleshy hand on his shoulder. He turned around to see Mr Charles filling the doorway.

When did everyone around here get so big, thought Indra to himself. He turned back to the woman from MI5. 'I'm sorry, you took the Prime Minister where? Because if you know where he is then—'

'The Prime Minister's car seems to have disappeared, sir,' said Mr Charles. 'There's no record of it.'

Indra really was baffled now. So the Prime Minister was actually missing?

Joseph Green nodded. 'Tell me everything.' Then he looked at Indra. 'Off you pop, sweet pea.'

Before he turned to leave, Indra realised two things. Firstly, he knew that the Prime Minister hadn't had a car booked that morning. He was scheduled to have breakfast with the Queen and then wall-to-wall meetings with various MPs. So why would Margaret Blaine have escorted him to a car?

The second thing he realised was that Oliver Charles's hand was still on his shoulder. He turned and looked up at him.

Oliver Charles smiled down at him.

Joseph Green farted.

Margaret Blaine giggled.

Indra Ganesh smiled politely and quickly left the Prime Minister's office.

Outside the office, he paused. Something was going on and he needed to work out who he should talk to. He decided to see what else the Emergency Protocols had to say and then he would work out who he could trust. Because he was pretty certain that he did not trust the new acting Prime Minister of the United Kingdom.

At Albion Hospital, Toshiko Sato sat in her chair, holding her handbag, and she waited for the Doctor. Suddenly she heard a single scratching sound, like a nail down a blackboard. Then silence. She sat back and tried to relax. She had a mission to concentrate on. It must have just been a mouse.

Then the scratching started again.

And then, with horror, Toshiko realised that the scratching was coming from inside the locker. The locker containing the dead alien.

6

Barry's Great Escape

'And where do you think you're going?' hollered Rose as she strode across the courtyard of the Powell Estate.

The Doctor was pushing open the door to the TARDIS. He stopped and turned to face Rose. 'Nowhere. It's just a bit human in there for me. History just happened and they're talking about where you can buy dodgy top-up cards for half price. I'm off on a wander, that's all.'

Rose shook her head. 'There's a spaceship in the Thames and you're just wandering.'

'Nothing to do with me,' the Doctor replied with a shrug. 'It's not an invasion. That was a genuine crash landing. Angle of descent, colour of smoke, everything. It's perfect.'

Then, looking around at the Powell Estate, at the flats and the people and the pets and the dodgy top-up cards, he said, 'Maybe this is it. First Contact. The day mankind officially comes into contact with an alien race. I'm not interfering because you've got to handle this on your own.' He turned and stared at Rose. 'That's when the human race finally grows up. Just this morning you were all tiny and small and made of clay. Now you can expand.'

He turned back to the TARDIS as Rose considered what he had just said. *This is the day that everything changes*, she thought. *You've got to handle this on your own*. Was he leaving her? She felt as if she was choking, as if she was going to burst into tears, as if the world had ended. She forced a smile, not wanting to scare the Doctor away.

'Promise you won't disappear?'

For what felt like eternity he stood with his back towards her, looking into the impossible world of his TARDIS. She wanted to plead, to beg him not to leave her, but she wouldn't do that. Then, slowly, he turned. He was holding something in his hand.

A key.

'Tell you what,' he said, casually. 'TARDIS key. It's about time you had one. See you later.'

He threw the key at Rose, and she caught it and she realised that she would never – and *could* never, ever – leave the Doctor. He stepped into the TARDIS, and she watched it disappear.

But she *knew* he would come back. For her.

With the biggest grin, Rose Tyler put the key into her pocket and headed back towards the stairwell.

Up above, on the top floor of the Powell Estate, Mickey Smith, who had been clearing up the broken glass from his window, stared down into the courtyard. The TARDIS. The Doctor. Rose. He stared, struggling to take it all in, then he started to run.

Toshiko Sato stared at the locker. The scratching continued. The alien had been dead; she was certain of it. She tried not to panic. Should she call her colleagues at Torchwood? She knew they'd tell her to concentrate on the mission. But her natural curiosity meant she had to know what was happening in the locker. She stood up and started to move towards it . . .

Indra Ganesh had his head in his hands, and he was very much trying not to sob. The acting Prime Minister had told him not to interrupt him with any calls or messages but every leader in the world was trying to speak to him, and now every leader in the world was taking it out on Indra. He'd read all of the Emergency Protocols but there was nothing in them about what to do if you just, well, simply didn't like or trust the acting Prime Minister you'd just enabled.

He knew that General Asquith would be returning from Albion Hospital shortly. He didn't particularly like the General. The man was old school, with very old-fashioned views on, well, anyone who wasn't a straight white man who'd been to a posh school. *But*, Indra mused, *I think he can be trusted . . .*

There was a knock at his door.

'What now?' he asked.

The door opened and there stood Harriet Jones with a cup of coffee. She smiled at him and suddenly he found himself thinking of his mother. She must be terrified, what with everything that was happening. He decided he would call her later.

Harriet walked over to him, closing the door behind her. 'I bet no one's brought you a cup of coffee,' she said as she placed it on his desk.

'Thank you,' he replied, genuinely grateful. Then he looked up with a friendly grin. 'You still can't see the PM.'

'Damn.' She winked and smiled back at him. 'You've seen through my cunning plan.'

'I'm sorry.' He took a sip of the coffee. 'It's just impossible.'

'Not even for two minutes? I don't get many chances to walk these corridors, I'm just a faithful backbencher. And I know we've had a brave new world land right on our doorstep, and that's wonderful ...' She hesitated. 'I think that's probably wonderful. Nevertheless, ordinary life keeps ticking away. I need to enter this paper.'

Indra genuinely had no idea how to respond to Harriet's passionate speech. Suddenly, his door was shoved open so roughly that it nearly came off its hinges. The new Prime Minister stood in the doorway.

'You. Short one.' He pointed at Indra. 'Where is the high chief of the army?'

'Do you mean General Asquith, sir?' Indra tried to keep the irritation out of his voice. 'Chief of the Defence Staff?'

'That's what I said.'

'He's on his way back from Albion Hospital, sir,' Indra replied. 'He's already developed some proposals with regards to containing the situation.'

'Good, good. Tall fellow, isn't he?'

Indra stared at him. 'Sir?'

'Asquith, big man? Tall, broad?'

Indra looked at Harriet then back at the Prime Minister. 'Erm ... yes, sir.'

'Good, good.' The Prime Minister turned to leave.

Harriet suddenly spoke up, bringing out a folder from her bag. 'Oh, Mr Green, sir. I know you're busy, but could you put this on the next Cabinet agenda?'

The Prime Minister didn't turn back. 'What is it?'

'Cottage hospitals. I've worked out a system whereby cottage hospitals do not have to be excluded from centres of excellence. You see, my mother's in the Flydale infirmary. That's my constituency. Tiny little place, you wouldn't know it.'

The Prime Minister suddenly roared. 'By all the saints, get some perspective, woman! I'm busy.'

He stomped off back towards his office. Indra and Harriet stared at each other, stunned at the man's behaviour.

'Damn.' Indra jumped up. 'I forgot to give him this!' He grabbed hold of the Emergency Protocols and stood up.

'What is it?' asked Harriet.

'The Emergency Protocols. Details the actions to be taken by the Government of Great Britain in the event of an alien incursion.' Indra wasn't really sure he should give them to Joseph Green, but the law was the law. Until he could speak to General Asquith, he'd continue to do his job and follow the rules.

He was about to head out when his telephone started to ring. He answered it.

'Yes, sir.' He covered the mouth of the telephone with his hand and looked up at Harriet. 'President Winters,' he explained.

'Horrible man, never liked him,' she replied. She indicated the red box. 'Why don't I take this to the Prime Minister? I promise not to even once mention cottage hospitals.'

Indra nodded as the President of the United States of America hollered down the telephone at him.

Outside Indra's office, Harriet Jones, MP for Flydale North, put her quickly devised plan into action. She opened the box and placed her folder proposal inside with the Emergency Protocols. She smiled to herself as she headed down the corridor towards the Prime Minister's office. He absolutely would read her proposal. Then she opened the box again and looked down at the Emergency Protocols. Just what was the Government supposed to do during an alien incursion, she wondered.

Toshiko Sato stared at the locker as she moved closer towards it. Closer. Closer. Suddenly, the scratching became a banging. *Thump! Thump! Thump!* Something – the alien, the thing that had crashed into Big Ben – was trying to get out.

It was alive.

Toshiko kept moving closer . . .

She reached out with a hand. It was like being in a nightmare. She wanted to run but she couldn't.

She had to open the locker. As her fingers brushed lightly against the cold metal of the locker door, it burst open. The handle flew off, hitting Toshiko's forehead, and she fell back, staring up in horror as the thing jumped out from inside the locker and scampered out of the room. Dazed, her forehead bleeding, Toshiko staggered to her feet and ran over to the wall, slamming her hand on an emergency alarm button. A siren started to blare out throughout Albion Hospital. The door swung open as a man entered.

'You rang?' he asked.

Toshiko looked up and gasped. It was him. The Doctor. The reason she had come to London. But all she could think about right now was the alien.

'It's alive,' she told him.

Soldiers were swarming into the room, but the Doctor quickly turned to face them. 'Defence plan delta! Come on, move! Move!'

The soldiers immediately turned and ran. The Doctor looked down at Tosh and held out his hand. She took it and he helped her back to her feet. She looked up and –

She stared into his eyes, and it was as if the world stopped turning.

'Are you all right?' he asked her, gently. She nodded. His eyes burned with compassion and hope and fear and love. The Doctor.

Then suddenly he let go of her hand and started to run. 'Tell the perimeter it's a lockdown!' he called back at her. But Toshiko ignored his instructions and chased after him down the corridor. 'I swear it was dead!'

'Coma, shock, hibernation, anything,' the Doctor called back. 'What does it look like?'

Then he stopped and looked at an innocent-looking filing cabinet. Toshiko caught up with him and stopped. He quickly mouthed at her to stay quiet.

They both stared at the filing cabinet as the door started to slowly open.

A pink ear appeared first. Followed ever-so-slowly by a pink cheek, a black eye, a pink snout.

'Hello,' said the Doctor to the pig. 'Who are you, then?'

The pig oinked.

'Barry?' replied the Doctor. 'It's nice to meet you.'

The pig stepped out of the filing cabinet then stopped, frozen, terrified as soldiers appeared at the end of the corridor.

The pig ran. The Doctor ran after it. The universe never stopped being full of surprises.

A young soldier, leaving one of the rooms, turned to see the pig running towards him. Terrified, he quickly raised his rifle and shot the animal cleanly through its skull.

Barry the pig, who had once dreamed of adventures in the stars, dreamed no more.

The Doctor ran over to the pig's body.

'What did you do that for? It was scared! It was scared.'

Toshiko watched as the Doctor started to cry. It broke her heart.

General Ronald Asquith was striding down a corridor in 10 Downing Street and he was angry. He was furious. The young fellow had told him about how the Prime Minister was missing and about how Joseph Green was now in charge. And how nothing was being done. Nothing at all was getting done on this, the most important day in human history! He reached the Prime Minister's office. A plain-looking woman was standing outside holding the Emergency Protocols.

'Can I help you, madam?'

The woman gave him a friendly smile. 'Harriet Jones, MP for Flydale North.'

'And?'

'And I came here to give the Prime Minister the Emergency Protocols.' She held up the box. 'I didn't read them,' she added, in a tone that suggested she absolutely had read them.

General Asquith stared at the unimportant woman, took the box, opened the door and entered the Prime Minister's office.

In the mortuary at Albion Hospital, Toshiko Sato and the Doctor looked down at the body of the pig. He seemed confused as to how easily she had been tricked. Did he suspect she wasn't really a doctor?

'I just assumed that's what aliens look like,' she said with a weak smile. 'But you're saying it's an ordinary pig from Earth?'

'More like a mermaid,' the Doctor replied. 'Victorian showmen used to draw the crowds by taking the skull of a cat, gluing it to a fish and calling it a mermaid. Now someone's taken a pig, opened up its brain, stuck bits on, then they've strapped it in that ship and made it dive bomb. It must've been terrified. They've taken this animal and turned it into a joke.'

Toshiko flinched. The Doctor's rage was quiet and still but terrifying. 'But the technology augmenting its brain, it's like nothing on Earth. It's alien. Aliens are faking aliens. Why would they do that? Doctor?'

But the Doctor was running.

She followed him out of the room, but he was gone.

Toshiko stood in the corridor, and she had no idea what to do. The Torchwood Institute's main objective was to protect the United Kingdom from threats of extraterrestrial origin including – and especially – the man known as the Doctor. Jack, the head of the Welsh branch of Torchwood, had a different, personal agenda.

'It's complicated,' he had once told his team. 'I don't want us to capture the Doctor. I can't even meet him. I want to so much but I can't. But if he's on Earth, and I can make it happen, then one of you will. And you will protect him with your life.'

Toshiko checked that the gun – given to her to protect the Doctor – was still in her handbag. Then she slowly walked down the corridor, towards the exit of the hospital. She may have lost the Doctor, but she had finally met him, and he had been *everything*. She felt different, as if just meeting him had changed something inside her. Despite everything that was happening today she felt just that little bit more alive.

She stepped out into the sunshine and pushed through the crowd of soldiers and news reporters. As she walked down the busy street, towards

Limehouse Green Station, she wondered just how many lives the Doctor had changed ...

Mickey Smith stood outside the front door of 48 Bucknall House on the Powell Estate, and he listened to the muffled sound of the party coming from inside the flat.

He heard Jackie Tyler call out, 'Here's to the Martians!' He heard everyone else cheer.

He stood there, trying to summon up the courage to ring the doorbell.

He stood there, his finger hovering over the doorbell as he remembered everything.

A year ago, he'd been kidnapped by an alien disguised as a wheelie bin and taken to a furnace underneath the London Eye. He'd been rescued by his girlfriend and this man called the Doctor, then the Doctor and Rose Tyler had gone off and left him.

People had assumed that he'd hurt Rose. Even his best mates had started to doubt his innocence. Mickey's life had become a living hell. To make things worse, the Government had lied. Everyone thought there'd been some kind of gas leak. When he tried to tell anyone about the Doctor and about him being an alien, they'd just laughed. 'There's no such things as aliens,' people would say. Well, he thought, they won't be saying that after today!

Mickey inched his finger closer to the doorbell...

But it wasn't just Rose the Doctor had taken from Mickey. The police had long ago confirmed that he wasn't a person of interest in the disappearance of Rose Tyler and, over time, everyone had come to accept this.

Except for one person. Jackie Tyler.

And it hurt so much. Jackie had watched him grow up. She'd been good friends with his nan. She'd been good friends with Mickey himself, but she hadn't believed him when he'd tried to tell her about the Doctor. Nobody had. Because the Government had said there was no such thing as aliens.

And now Mickey had seen that Rose was back. And nobody had even bothered to tell him.

He decided not to ring the doorbell. Instead, he shoved the door open and Mickey Smith crashed the party.

General Ronald Asquith was shouting at the Prime Minister.

He'd never shouted at a Prime Minister before. He wasn't a huge fan of the missing Prime Minister, who was far too fond of political correctness and pop psychology for his liking, but even that delicate little lightweight was more suited to the job than the sweaty behemoth standing in front of him.

'I've got the White House phoning me direct because Downing Street won't answer their calls,' he raged at Joseph Green. 'This is outrageous! We haven't even started the vaccination programme. This is appalling. The nations of the world are watching the United Kingdom.'

He looked over at Margaret Blaine and Oliver Charles, urging them to back him up.

Joseph Green only smirked. 'Well, it has all been a bit of a shock.'

Asquith continued his rant. 'This is the greatest crisis in modern history, and you've done nothing. Your behaviour has been shameful, sir. You're supposed to be in charge. We need positive leadership. The capital's ground to a halt.'

He looked again at Blaine and Charles, but they just stood there, watching him. Silent.

Asquith continued. 'Furthermore, we can only assume that the Prime Minister's disappearance is the direct result of hostile alien action, and what have you been doing? Nothing.' Asquith wondered why the rest of the Cabinet hadn't returned from the conference in Brighton. He made a mental note to ask that little Indian fellow as soon as possible.

Joseph Green stared down at Asquith and something about the look in his eyes unnerved the General.

'Sorry,' said Green, quietly. 'I thought I was Prime Minister now.'

'Only by default,' replied General Asquith. He was about to start outlining his plans for dealing with the situation when Joseph Green stepped closer towards him. General Asquith was a tall man, and he wasn't used to having to look up at someone. He looked up as Joseph Green smiled down at him.

'Oh, that's not fair,' said the Prime Minister. 'I've been having such fun.'

General Asquith was appalled. 'You think this is fun?'

'It's a hoot,' replied the Prime Minister.

'Honestly, it's super,' said Margaret Blaine, who had moved and was now standing behind General Asquith. She started to giggle.

And then, to General Asquith's horror, Oliver Charles farted. The Prime Minister and Oliver Charles joined in with Margaret Blaine's giggling.

'Oh, excuse me,' said Charles as he farted again.

General Asquith couldn't process what was happening. Had they all been drugged? 'What's going on here? Where's the rest of the Cabinet? Why haven't they been airlifted in?'

'I cancelled it,' replied the Prime Minister, taking another step closer to the General. Asquith found himself gagging on the stench of Joseph Green's breath as the man continued. 'They'd only get in the way.'

And then the Prime Minister farted too, as did Margaret Blaine from MI5.

She giggled. 'I'm shaking my booty!'

General Ronald Asquith looked around him at the three giggling imbeciles. 'Sir,' he addressed the Prime Minister. 'Under Section Five of the Emergency Protocols, it is my duty to relieve you of command. And by God, I'll put this country under martial law if I have to.'

The Prime Minister placed a huge hand on the General's shoulder and whispered in his ear, 'Oh, I'm scared.' He stood back and raised his huge hand up to his huge sweaty forehead. 'I mean, that's hair-raising. Literally, look!'

General Ronald Asquith couldn't do anything but look. He stared up as the Prime Minister of the United Kingdom began to unzip his forehead. Blue light poured out from under Joseph Green's skin. Through the light, Ronald could just about see a face. A broad, alien face. Big black eyes staring out at him. They blinked.

General Ronald Theodore Asquith suddenly realised that the pig he'd seen at Albion Hospital had just been a pig. And in his final seconds he worked out what the creatures in front of him had planned. The swine, the spaceship, Big Ben. It all made sense. Then, he remembered that time he'd stood on the moon's surface and he'd looked out into space at the planet Earth. It had looked so small and fragile in the dark. He'd looked out at 6 billion people all just trying to live their lives with joy and love and now, seeing the creature revealing its true form in front of him, he knew that those 6 billion people were all going to die.

He looked at the creature's face as it smiled at him. He had never seen an alien before. It would be the last thing he ever would see.

Outside the room, stepping back from the keyhole, Harriet Jones, MP for Flydale North, covered her mouth to stop herself screaming at the horror she'd just witnessed. She was about to turn and run when something made her stop and keep watching.

Through the keyhole, she watched as the big blond man standing next to what had been the acting Prime Minister unzipped his forehead. She watched as he unzipped his whole body. She watched as the thing that had been inside of him then stepped out of the big blond man's skin and she watched what happened next.

Then, she stopped watching and she started to run.

7

Somebody Owes Mickey an Apology

Mickey Smith stood in the doorway of the living room of the Tylers' flat. Everyone had fallen silent and was looking at him.

Rose stood up slowly. 'I was going to come and see you.'

'Somebody owes Mickey an apology,' said Ru quietly.

Everyone turned to look at Jackie. She was standing in the middle of the room, carrying a plate piled high with cocktail sausages. 'Well, it's not my fault,' she said, sounding guilty. 'Be fair. What was I supposed to think?'

Mickey then turned to look directly at Rose and nodded. She gave him a small nod of understanding and followed him out of the flat. Jackie, handing the plate to Ru, went after them.

Outside, in the courtyard, Mickey stared at the two Tyler women. A year before, everything had been good. Mickey and his girlfriend, Rose, and her mother, his friend, Jackie. Everything had changed and now it was like he was looking at two strangers. He waited for Rose to say something, but she was busy looking anywhere except at him.

Then, not caring who heard him, Mickey started to shout, his voice echoing around the courtyard of the Powell Estate. 'You disappear, who do they turn to? Your boyfriend. Five times I was taken in for questioning. Five times. No evidence. Course, there couldn't be, could there? And then I get her, your mother, whispering around the estate, pointing the finger. Stuff through my letterbox, and all cos of you.' He paused for breath but before he could continue, Rose spoke.

'I didn't think I'd be gone so long,' she said quietly.

'And I waited for you, Rose. Twelve months, waiting for you and the Doctor to come back.'

'Hold on.' Jackie turned on him. 'You knew about the Doctor? Why didn't you tell me?'

Mickey wanted to scream. He had tried so many times to tell Jackie, but she had refused to listen to him. He had tried to tell the police, but they had refused to listen to him. The whole world had refused to listen to him and his stories about the northern bloke with the time-travelling police box. What was the point? No longer caring whether Rose had an explanation, he turned to her with a bitter sneer.

'Anyway,' he said, 'the Doctor's gone. That box thing just faded away.'

Mickey started to walk away from the Tylers.

Rose felt sorry for Mickey. She felt sorry for what he must have been through, and she felt sorry for him now. She knew he was just trying to hurt her, but she knew the Doctor was coming back.

Mickey continued, calling back to her, 'Oh, he's dumped you, Rose. Sailed off into space. How does it feel, huh? Now you're left behind with the rest of us Earthlings. Get used to it.' His voice was now a vicious snarl, and it devastated Rose. Mickey wasn't cruel, he'd never been cruel. But she shook her head. She knew the Doctor was coming back. She knew it.

'He's not gone,' she said gently, more to herself than to Mickey. She reached into her pocket and took out the TARDIS key. She held it up as Mickey turned to look back at her and Jackie. 'Because he gave me this. He's not my boyfriend, Mickey. He's better than that. He's much more important than that.'

The TARDIS key suddenly began to glow. Rose, Mickey and Jackie stared at it. Wind started to build up, howling around the courtyard. Rose realised she could hear the distant sound of the TARDIS starting to materialise. She felt stupid but she didn't want her mum here for this. This was her thing.

'Mum! Mum, go inside.'

But Jackie, like Mickey, was staring as the blue police box started to slowly appear and disappear in front of them. 'Mum, don't stand there, just go inside. Just, Mum, go. Oh, blimey.'

The TARDIS appeared and solidified in front of them. It stood there as if it had always been standing there.

'How'd you do that, then?' Jackie asked her daughter. Rose almost wanted to laugh. Her mum presumably thought it was some kind of cheap magic trick.

The TARDIS door opened, and the Doctor stepped out. He saw Rose. 'I didn't just go for a wander.' He smiled sheepishly. 'All right, so I lied. I went and had a look. But the whole crash landing's a fake. I thought so. Just too perfect. I mean, hitting Big Ben – come on! So, I thought, let's go and have a look.'

Rose waited for him to notice Mickey and Jackie. Then, she ran into the TARDIS, pulling the Doctor in with her. She quickly went to close the door behind her, but Mickey Smith pushed his way through the doors, past her and into the spaceship.

In the Prime Minister's office at 10 Downing Street, the alien wearing the skin of Joseph Green shook the hand of the alien now wearing the skin of General Ronald Asquith. He took the discarded skin of Oliver Charles, emptied his pockets and went to hang it in a nearby cupboard.

'What do you think?' asked the General. 'How's the compression? I think I've got too much ballast round the middle.' He noisily released some air, trying to compress himself more into the skinsuit. 'Oh, that's better.'

Margaret Blaine giggled. 'We've really got to fix the gas exchange. It's getting ridiculous.'

Joseph Green smiled. 'I don't know. Seems very human to me.'

'Shame,' General Asquith smirked. 'I quite enjoyed being Oliver. He had a wife, a mistress and a young farmer.'

The Prime Minister went to the door and opened it. 'Back to work.'

The General nodded. 'I have an army to command.'

The three aliens smiled. They now controlled the Government and the army. They had near enough complete control of the United Kingdom. And the world was watching ...

It was time for the next phase of their operation.

Mickey looked around the TARDIS. He'd been in there once before, after the Doctor and Rose had rescued him from the monstrosity underneath the London Eye. He'd been in a state of shock then so hadn't really been able to comprehend quite what he'd been seeing. But now? He'd been waiting for this; he was making sure he took it all in so he could write about it on his website. Being in the TARDIS was like being in a cathedral, it was so huge. The walls were green and glowing. There was a mushroom of wires, cables, buttons and screens sprouting out from the middle of the floor. It was impossible. It was beautiful. It was terrifying and it was also, very clearly, somehow alive.

Mickey turned to rage at the Doctor. 'You ruined my life, Doctor. They thought she was dead. I was a murder suspect because of you.'

The Doctor ignored him and spoke to Rose. 'You see what I mean? Domestic.'

Mickey roared at him! 'I bet you don't even remember my name!'

The Doctor smiled at Rose. 'Ricky.'

Mickey wanted to punch him. 'It's Mickey!'

'No, it's Ricky.'

'I think I know my own name.'

'You *think* you know your own name?' The Doctor turned to him. 'How stupid are you?'

Mickey clenched his fists. He had had enough. He started to run at the Doctor.

Then a small, quiet, confused gasp made Mickey stop. He, the Doctor and Rose all turned to look at the doors leading out to the Powell Estate.

Jackie Tyler was standing in the doorway looking into the TARDIS.

Everyone stood still for a few seconds and then Jackie turned and started to run. Rose ran after her.

Outside the TARDIS, Rose grabbed Jackie's arm. 'Mum, it's not like that. He's not—'

Jackie stared at her. 'Alien?' She pulled away from her daughter and began to walk back towards the stairwell.

Rose moved to go after her but was torn. The Doctor had said the spaceship crash was faked. What was happening? The sun was starting to set over London as Rose Tyler stood in the middle of the Powell Estate courtyard. She turned to look at the TARDIS, green light shining out through the doors. She turned back to look at her terrified mum as she started to climb the stairs leading back up to the flat.

Which way should she go? The TARDIS or home?

Harriet Jones had been hiding in the toilets at 10 Downing Street for over an hour. She wasn't ashamed that she'd had a little cry about what she had seen, but now she needed to work out what to do next. She knew she had two choices. She could quietly stand up, leave the toilets, walk down the corridor and leave the building. She could then get a bus to Victoria train station and get the first train back to Flydale North. She could go home, she could call her mother, she could feed her cat, Winifred, and she could watch the rest of the day's events unfold on television.

She could do that. That would, she knew, be the sensible thing to do.

She was smiling to herself, thinking of home, when suddenly she remembered the giant claw slicing down, slicing down and through General Ronald Asquith, as the Prime Minister's office filled with that blinding blue light. She shook her head, trying to push away the image she already knew would haunt her nightmares. She tried to think of reasons why she should leave this horrible, terrible situation to someone else. She should let someone important deal with it.

Then, she remembered the giggling. Those inhuman creatures giggling as they ended a man's life.

Harriet Jones, MP for Flydale North, knew she had to do something. She thought about the information she'd read in the Emergency Protocols. Apparently, there existed a secret military organisation, the Unified Intelligence Taskforce, known as UNIT. They'd dealt with alien invasions before – who knew, thought Harriet, that the Earth had even been invaded before? The first port of call was a Major Thomas Richard Blake at UNIT HQ, which was apparently under the Tower of London. Harriet hadn't thought, when reading the documents, to memorise the phone number. She didn't know London very well so she wondered how long it would take her to get to the Tower. There'd also been information about a second organisation, Torchwood, which had bases in Cardiff and Canary Wharf, here in London. There wasn't as much information about Torchwood; the protocols had stated that the Government didn't officially know that Torchwood existed and that the Institute should only be contacted if UNIT was out of action. Harriet had sighed, reading that. There was always so much red tape and silliness to deal with in politics, apparently even in the case of an alien invasion.

There had also been a third option in the protocols. Something known as Code Nine that merely stated: 'Find the Doctor.'

Harriet stood up. She wished she had one of those fancy new phones that had the internet on it, but she'd never really got on with technology. This meant she'd have to ask someone for directions to the Tower of London. She wanted to trust that nice young Mr Ganesh, but she wasn't sure she could really trust anyone.

The alien had put on General Asquith's skin like a coat. Anyone in Downing Street could be an alien.

Harriet washed her hands and glanced at her reflection. She forced herself to look strong and determined. If she looked strong and determined, then hopefully she would feel it on the inside. Suddenly the door opened and she yelped. Two young women entered. One went into one of the cubicles as the other stood next to Harriet and started to reapply her lipstick.

'I mean, finally,' called out the woman from the cubicle. 'At least they're finally doing something.'

'I know,' said the woman next to Harriet. 'Finally!'

Harriet gave her a pleasant smile. 'Harriet Jones, MP for Flydale North. Sorry, who's finally doing something?'

'The Prime Minister.' She finished applying her lipstick, smacked her lips together and pursed them. 'He's getting together all the world's top alien experts and bringing them here. They're going to have a conference.'

'Which means,' said the woman in the cubicle. 'I need to order in about fifty extra sandwiches. And you can guarantee half of these experts will be vegan.'

'Oh, I know,' her friend called back to her. 'Bloody vegans, they'll be the end of us all.'

But Harriet Jones was no longer listening. As she left the toilets she had just one thing on her mind. Why on earth would an alien pretending to be the Prime Minister call the world's top alien experts to Downing Street?

Mickey was staring at the Doctor, who was staring at a graphic of the spaceship crashing into Big Ben. They'd been standing in silence since Rose had left to chase after Jackie. Now she came back, barging in through the TARDIS doors.

'The thing I don't understand ...' Rose ran right up to the Doctor and stood next to him. Mickey's chest nearly burst at the sight. They looked so right, the Doctor and Rose. They were in sync. 'The thing I don't understand – that was a real spaceship.'

'Yep,' replied the Doctor.

Mickey decided to speak up. 'Funny way to invade, putting the world on red alert.'

There was a pause then the Doctor and Rose both turned to look at him. Rose smiled and Mickey's heart skipped a beat.

'Good point,' replied the Doctor. 'So, what're they up to?' He started to fiddle with buttons and switches on the console.

Rose came over to Mickey. 'I *am* sorry,' she said softly.

Mickey felt tears in his eyes and tried so hard to stop them. 'Every day, I looked. On every street corner, wherever I went, looking for a blue box for a whole year.'

Rose took his hand in hers. 'It's only been a few days for me. I don't know. It's hard to tell inside this thing but I swear it's just a few days since I left you.'

Mickey gently squeezed her hand and gave her an awkward grin. 'Not enough time to miss me, then?'

'I did miss you. So, erm, in twelve months have you been seeing anyone else?'

'No.'

'Okay.'

'Mainly because everyone thinks I murdered you.'

'Right.'

There was an awkward pause then Mickey asked the question he'd been dying to ask since he'd first seen her at the party. 'So, now that you've come back, are you going to stay?'

Before Rose could answer, the Doctor turned to them. 'Got it!'

Rose went to join him, looking at the monitor. Mickey followed.

'Patched in the radar,' the Doctor explained. 'Looped it back twelve hours so we can follow the flight of that spaceship. Here we go.'

The graphic on the monitor changed. The Doctor explained what they were looking at.

'That's the spaceship on its way to Earth, see? Except. Hold on.' The graphic of the spaceship showed the trajectory changing. 'See?' Mickey did not see. 'The spaceship did a slingshot around the Earth before it landed.'

Mickey looked at Rose and shrugged.

'What does that mean?' Rose asked the Doctor.

The Doctor grinned. 'It means it came from Earth in the first place. It went up and came back down. Whoever those aliens are, they haven't just arrived, they've been here for a while. The question is, what have they been doing?'

Jackie Tyler sat in her living room. Alone. Again.

Lovely Molly from downstairs had shooed out the other guests and had asked Jackie if she wanted company. Jackie had just shaken her head and thanked her.

Now she was alone. Rose had chosen the Doctor over her.

She switched the television back on. Reporters were jostling outside 10 Downing Street as more and more apparently very important people were let into the building.

As she watched, the BBC reporter turned to face the camera. 'Are there more ships to come? And what is their intention? The authorities are now asking if anyone knows anything.'

Jackie stood up. She walked over to the window and looked down into the courtyard. She looked down at the blue box standing there as if it had always stood there. Light from the windows of the box was shining out across the courtyard like a beacon. She listened as the reporter continued.

'If any previous sightings have been made, then call this number. We need your help.'

Harriet Jones was hiding in a store cupboard, squashed up against a mop and bucket. She kept pushing open the door and peeking out, watching Mr Ganesh. He was rushing around, welcoming various very important people. He seemed to be trustworthy but something was bothering Harriet, and she couldn't put her finger on it. Some connection. Something she'd seen.

She watched as Mr Ganesh effortlessly slid in between two other Downing Street employees to welcome an astronaut she'd once seen on television. The astronaut, she couldn't remember his name, was a big chap. Mr Ganesh started to shake his hand.

Harriet gasped as she worked it out! The aliens disguised as humans were big. The acting Prime Minister was huge! They were big because the aliens had to fit inside them. Mr Ganesh wasn't a big man. Presumably an alien couldn't fit inside his skin. Which meant, Harriet hoped, he could be trusted. She might have an ally to help her defeat this alien invasion of Earth. *Logic*, she thought. *Even in this terrible, strange situation, logic wins.*

'How many channels do you get?'

Mickey, Rose and the Doctor were now watching BBC News on the TARDIS's monitor.

'All the basic packages,' the Doctor replied.

'You get sports channels?' Mickey heard Rose snort with laughter. She'd always found his football obsession amusing. Mickey hoped the question was reminding her of how things used to be. Football in the pub with his mates. The good old days.

'Hold on,' said the Doctor. 'I know that lot.'

Mickey looked at the monitor. A group of people in dark blue uniforms were entering 10 Downing Street.

'UNIT. Unified Intelligence Taskforce,' said the Doctor. 'Good people.'

'How do you know them?' asked Rose.

'Cos he's worked for them,' Mickey replied, smugly. He enjoyed Rose's shock that he might know something about her precious Doctor that she didn't. 'Oh, yeah, don't think I sat on my backside for twelve months, Doctor. I read up on you. You look deep enough on the internet or in the history books, and there's his name. Followed by a list of the dead.'

'That's nice. Good boy, Ricky.'

The Doctor didn't look bothered, but Mickey suspected he had got under his skin. He imagined the football commentary: *Mickey Smith – 1. The Doctor and Rose – 0.*

Rose turned back to the Doctor. 'If you know them, why don't you go and help?'

'They wouldn't recognise me. I've changed a lot since the old days. Besides, the world's on a knife-edge. There's aliens out there and fake aliens. We want to keep *this* alien out of the mix. I'm going undercover.' The Doctor turned to Mickey. 'Ricky, you've got a car. You can do some driving.'

'Where to?'

The Doctor grinned and strode down the TARDIS ramp towards the doors. Rose followed the Doctor, and Mickey followed Rose. The Doctor flung open the TARDIS doors and they stepped back out into the courtyard.

A bright white light suddenly shone down on them and, looking up, Mickey could see a helicopter. Then he realised they were surrounded. Police cars, sirens, guns. The TARDIS was surrounded.

'Raise your hands above your head,' shouted a voice. 'You are under arrest.'

The Doctor raised his hands and grinned. 'Take me to your leader.'

As Rose raised her hands, Mickey ran.

Harriet Jones was just leaving the store cupboard when she saw the fake General Asquith and Margaret Blaine stomping towards Mr Ganesh. Mr Ganesh was just ending a phone call and he looked up, clearly intimidated by the General.

'Sir,' said Mr Ganesh, his voice trembling. 'We've had a priority alarm. It's Code Nine. Confirmed Code Nine.'

Harriet remembered what she'd read in the Emergency Protocols. They must have found the Doctor.

'Code Nine?' asked Asquith.

Mr Ganesh looked confused. Harriet realised that Mr Ganesh knew that the General should really know what Code Nine was. 'In the event of the Emergency Protocols being activated, we've got software that automatically searches all communications for key words, and one of those words is Doctor. I think we've found him, sir.'

Harriet breathed a sigh of relief. The Doctor was being brought to Downing Street. Doctors always made things better. She wondered if he worked in a cottage hospital . . .

PC Tristan White sipped from a polystyrene cup of lukewarm coffee as he leant against his car. The courtyard of the Powell Estate was almost empty now. The mysterious Doctor and Rose Tyler had been taken away. Police tape had been wrapped round the strange blue box they'd been hiding in. A couple of Tristan's colleagues, Emma and Andi, were checking behind the bins for Mickey Smith but otherwise, for the first time that day, Tristan was finally alone. It had been a long day. His shift should have finished hours ago but because of the unfolding events everyone had been forced to do overtime. Even Janice on reception.

Tristan sipped his coffee and looked up at the moon. He wondered if the aliens had come from there. Wherever they'd come from, he just hoped they were friendly.

Tristan then became aware of something, someone, stepping into the courtyard from Jordan Road. The man, surely it was a man, was huge. The huge silhouette slowly, silently started to walk towards him. Tristan put the cup of coffee onto the car roof and stood up straight. He wasn't a big man, but he knew karate. He braced himself, ready for any trouble. The shadow was suddenly lit up by the moonlight and Tristan gasped.

'Terry?'

Assistant Commissioner Strickland, standing in the moonlight, smiled at him. Terry Strickland was a huge bear of man but was very much known for being a gentle giant. Tristan gave him a salute.

'What are you doing here, Terry?'

Terry Strickland approached Tristan and looked down at him. 'The woman who reported the Doctor. Jacqueline Tyler.'

Tristan nodded then recoiled as Terry breathed down. 'Crikey, Tel, what you been eating? Your old footy socks?'

Strickland just smiled. 'I'm here to see Jacqueline Tyler. To tidy up any loose ends.'

Tristan looked up at him. '48 Bucknall House,' he said, turning to point at a nearby stairwell. 'But listen, why don't I come with you?'

'Why?'

'I know them. Well, I met them this morning. Friendly face might help with the loose ends?'

'There's no need,' Strickland replied, smiling. Then he let one go noisily.

Tristan burst out laughing. 'Oh, mate, what is wrong with you? That's rank!'

Strickland giggled. Tristan had never seen him giggle before. It was bizarre. Terry was a big bloke with a big hearty laugh. Now he was giggling like Janice on reception.

'Let me come up,' said Tristan. 'Then we can sneak off for a pint.'

Strickland looked irritated. He looked around the deserted courtyard slowly. 'We are alone?'

Tristan nodded. He looked up, confused, as his old pal Terry Strickland slowly raised one of his big meaty arms up above him and –

'Oi, what are you two lovebirds up to?' PC Emma McLellan stepped out from behind the bins, followed shortly by PC Andi Reeves. 'No sign of Mickey Smith, I'm afraid.'

Strickland lowered his arm, looking down at the three police officers as they crowded around him.

'So,' asked Andi, with a cheeky grin. 'Who fancies a pint?'

'Terry's got to go and see Rose Tyler's mother but I'm free,' replied Tristan.

'*Excellente*,' replied Emma. 'Dodgy-looking place around the corner. Cheap though.'

Tristan moved to join them then patted Terry on his huge broad back. 'Good luck with Jackie Tyler, mate. She's quite something.'

The three police officers headed off back towards Jordan Road. The creature calling itself Assistant Commissioner Terry Strickland slowly turned back to the flats and looked up. High above him he could see the scared face of a woman looking down at him.

It was time to tidy up the loose ends.

8

Inside Downing Street

Rose looked out of the police car window as they drove across Westminster Bridge. She smiled, remembering how a few days ago – a *year* ago, she reminded herself – she and the Doctor had run across it just before defeating the Nestene Consciousness. Running across that bridge, she'd felt so alive for the first time in such a very long time. She looked out of the window and imagined that she could see the pair of them running. The Doctor and Rose at the very start of their adventures.

The car turned onto Parliament Street. The road was packed with people waving placards and police officers. Surrounding the Cenotaph there seemed to be two factions. One group were waving placards welcoming the aliens, the other lot were screaming that there was no room in Britain for aliens. Rose sighed. Sometimes, she wondered if she was really part of the same species as that particular lot.

'We're being escorted,' said the Doctor, pointing out the two other police cars that were now ahead of them. The crowds were moving to let them through.

'Where to?' asked Rose. She had a sneaky suspicion. She knew what road was coming up on the left.

'Where d'you think?' the Doctor replied with a grin. 'Downing Street.'

She had been right. 'You're kidding!'

'I'm not.'

'Ten Downing Street!'

'That's the one.'

'Oh, my god.' Rose was almost laughing now. She imagined Shireen's face when she found out about this. 'I'm going to 10 Downing Street! How come?'

The Doctor frowned. 'I hate to say it, but Mickey was right. Over the years I've visited this planet a lot of times, and I've been noticed.'

Rose realised why they were being escorted not arrested. 'Now they need you?'

The Doctor nodded. 'Like it said on the news. They're gathering experts in alien knowledge. And who's the biggest expert of the lot?'

Rose smiled then her eyes went so wide as she innocently gasped, 'Patrick Moore?'

His eyes narrowed. 'Apart from him.'

'Oh, don't you just love it,' she replied with a laugh.

The Doctor grinned back at her. 'I'm telling you. Lloyd George, he used to drink me under the table. Who's the Prime Minister now?'

Rose shrugged. 'How should I know? I missed a year.'

She looked back out of the window as the car turned left and drove through the open gates onto Downing Street. The road was packed with news reporters who parted for the cars. Rose held her breath as they approached the famous black door she'd seen on the telly so many times. The car pulled up and a policeman got out and opened the doors for them. Cameras flashed as Rose and the Doctor were escorted to the front door. The Doctor turned and waved at them. Rose couldn't help but laugh.

Seconds later, they were inside the famous building and Rose took the Doctor's hand. A young man approached them.

'Indra Ganesh, sir.'

'Oh, not "sir",' replied the Doctor. 'I'm most definitely not a "sir". I'm the Doctor.' He shook Indra's hand.

Rose, ignored, introduced herself anyway. 'Rose Tyler. You all right?'

Indra Ganesh smiled weakly at her as he handed the Doctor an ID card.

Rose looked at it, as the Doctor pinned it to his coat. 'Where'd you get that photo from, then?'

'I'm sorry,' Indra said to the Doctor, ignoring her question. 'Your companion doesn't have clearance.'

'I don't go anywhere without her.'

'You're the Code Nine, not her. I'm sorry, Doctor. She'll have to stay outside.'

The Doctor folded his arms across his chest. 'She's staying with me.'

'Look, even I don't have clearance to go in there.' Indra looked exhausted and close to tears. 'I can't let her in and that's a fact.'

Rose felt sorry for him. 'It's all right,' she said to the Doctor. 'You go.'

Before the Doctor could answer, an older woman came crashing out of what appeared to be a cupboard and stumbled over to them.

'Harriet Jones, MP, Flydale North.'

Rose grinned at her. There was something instantly likeable about Harriet Jones, MP, Flydale North.

'Excuse me,' asked Harriet. 'Are you the Doctor?'

'Sure.'

Indra turned to Harriet, clearly irritated. 'Not now. We're busy. Can't you go home?'

Harriet turned to face him and stood up straight. 'I just need a word in private.' She was making it very clear that she wouldn't, in fact, be going home.

Rose told the Doctor that she'd be fine. He gave her a gentle hug and allowed himself to be escorted into the next room.

'I'm going to have to leave you with security,' Indra said to Rose but, before he could do anything, Harriet had taken Rose by the arm and they were walking away.

'It's all right, I'll look after her,' she called back to Indra. 'Let me be of some use.' Then she whispered in Rose's ear, 'Walk with me, just keep walking...'

Rose kept walking. Harriet led her into a large room which Rose recognised. It was the Cabinet Room where the Prime Minister would have his big important meetings. It was empty.

'This friend of yours, he's an expert, is that right? He knows about aliens?'

Rose tried not to laugh. If only she knew! 'Why do you want to know?'

Suddenly, Harriet Jones burst into tears. Rose

instinctively grabbed her and hugged her as the older woman sobbed onto her shoulder.

Jackie Tyler looked through into the living room at the large policeman currently squashed into the armchair. 'You sure you don't want a tea? It's no bother. Coffee? I might have some biscuits somewhere. Had a few people round earlier. You know, cos of the spaceship. Ooh, you must have had a long day. I remember the riots, you know.'

As she pottered around the kitchen looking for any leftover biscuits, Jackie thought she heard the policeman in her living room fart. She decided to pretend she hadn't heard anything.

'So, Rose is all right, then? She's not in any trouble?' She gave up on her search and went back through into the living room.

The policeman smiled at her.

General Muriel Frost looked around the room of assembled experts and very quickly deduced which one was the Doctor. She had met him a few times during her career at UNIT and they'd always got on well. He usually wore much fancier clothes but there was no hiding that look in his eyes. The man, at the back of the room, in the battered leather jacket was most definitely the Doctor.

Muriel tried to stifle a yawn. It had been a long day. Major Blake had requested she and her team return to the UK from Geneva as soon as UNIT had detected the UFO. They'd immediately boarded a UNIT jet and flown into the secret airfield just outside of Crawley. They'd not even had time to check into a hotel. Perhaps, she thought with a smile, the Doctor would put them all up in his TARDIS.

She looked up as the acting Prime Minister, Joseph Green, entered the room and headed to a desk in front of them. He was followed by General Asquith. Muriel smiled up at Ronnie. They'd been friends and poker buddies for years. He was old-fashioned but a demon at cards. He walked right past her, ignoring her, and joined Joseph Green at the front of the room.

Muriel toyed with her ID card, wondering why he hadn't acknowledged her.

The General started to speak. 'Now, ladies and gentlemen, if I could have your attention, please. As you can see from the summaries in front of you, the alien ship had one porcine occupant.'

The man at the back of the room stood up. 'Of course, the really interesting bit happened three days ago, see, filed away under Any Other Business. The North Sea; a satellite detected a signal, a little blip of radiation, at one hundred fathoms, like there's something down there. You were just about to investigate and the next thing you know, this happens. Spaceships, pigs, massive diversion. From what?'

Muriel Frost smiled. This was definitely the Doctor. She looked forward to reuniting with him later.

Harriet laid the discarded skin of Oliver Charles out on the large table that dominated the room. She had taken Rose to the Prime Minister's office and retrieved the horrible thing from the cupboard as well as the Emergency Protocols. They'd then quickly returned to the Cabinet Room.

'They turned the body into a suit.' Harriet was telling Rose everything she had witnessed. 'A disguise for the thing inside!'

Rose nodded. 'It's all right. I believe you. It's alien. They must have some serious technology behind this. If we could find it, we could use it.'

Rose started to rush around the room, opening drawers and cupboards. Harriet, thankful to finally have an ally, joined in. Rose went to open a large cupboard standing in the corner when the main door to the Cabinet Room opened suddenly and both women jumped.

Indra Ganesh came striding in. 'Harriet, for god's sake! This has gone beyond a joke.'

Harriet, now believing that Indra could be trusted, was about to reply. The three of them could save the day together. But, as Harriet took a step towards him, Rose opened the cupboard door and screamed as the body of a man fell out.

Harriet and Indra joined her and they all stared down at the body.

'Oh, my god,' exclaimed Indra. Suddenly everything was starting to make a horrible, terrifying sort of sense. 'That's the Prime Minister.'

None of them heard the door to the Cabinet Room being gently closed.

But all three of them heard the giggling.

Jackie Tyler jumped up, suddenly remembering where she'd kept a secret stash of choc chip cookies. She went through into the kitchen, calling back to the police officer.

'It was bigger on the inside. I don't know. What do I know about spaceships?'

The policeman called through to her. 'That's what worries me. You see, this man is classified as trouble. Which means that anyone associated with him is trouble. And that's my job.'

With a 'Ha!' of satisfaction, Jackie found the choc chip cookies hidden behind the toaster. She turned back towards the living room and stopped. A strange blue light was pulsing through into the hallway.

'That's my job,' repeated the policeman from somewhere in the electric haze. 'Eliminating trouble.'

In the Cabinet Room, Rose, Harriet and Indra watched as Margaret Blaine slowly walked towards them.

'Oh! Has someone been naughty?' she asked. Then she giggled again.

She raised a hand to her forehead and began to unzip the skin . . .

Muriel watched as the Doctor strode to the front of the briefing room.

'If aliens fake an alien crash and an alien pilot,' he said, 'what do they get? Us. They get us.' He frowned. 'It's not a diversion, it's a trap.'

She felt a chill. A fake crash. A fake pilot. Them all gathered together in one room. She looked over at Ronnie Asquith, again wondering why he didn't recognise her. She was about to stand up when, without warning, the Prime Minister loudly broke wind.

'Excuse me,' said the Doctor. 'Do you mind not farting while I'm saving the world?'

'Would you rather silent but deadly?' replied the Prime Minister.

Then he reached up to his forehead and unzipped the skin. An unearthly blue light started to pulse out from the middle of his head.

Muriel jumped to her feet and raised a gun as an alien face started to emerge from the Prime Minister's body. To her horror, Ronnie Asquith was also shrugging off his human flesh to reveal something green and glistening underneath. The remnants of her old friend discarded on the floor made Muriel feel sick.

Harriet, Rose and Indra stared in horror as Margaret Blaine's skin dropped to the carpet in fleshy folds. An alien now stood before them. Over seven feet tall, green with huge black eyes and scaly claws for hands. Harriet stared at it and suddenly everything fell into place. Why would aliens want the world's leading alien experts at Downing Street?

It was so that they could –

Before she could say anything, the alien had launched itself over the table and was standing with them. As Harriet screamed, the alien wrapped a claw around Indra's neck and hoisted him up against the wall. Its other claw started scrabbling for Rose.

Jackie Tyler nervously walked back into her living room. She shielded her eyes; the blue light was so bright. Then, through the light, she made out the creature that stood where the policeman had been sitting. She started to scream.

Indra Ganesh hung from the claw as it slowly crushed his neck – the nightmarish end to the worst day of his life. Suddenly, he realised, nothing mattered. He just wished he'd got around to calling his mum. The last thing Indra Ganesh thought, as the final breath left his body, was that he wasn't really in love with Bob McCormack and that was really quite sad.

As panic broke out in the briefing room, Muriel aimed her gun at the creatures. But before she could call for the Doctor to join her, the monstrosity that had hidden inside Asquith spoke.

'We are the Slitheen,' it said. 'Thank you all for wearing your ID cards. They'll help to identify the bodies.'

The creature reached into the desk and pulled out a small, metallic cube. He crushed it in his huge claw and electricity arced out from inside, targeting the cards everybody wore pinned to their chests.

As the power surged through Muriel Frost's body and burned out her brain, she found herself wishing she had travelled with the Doctor. If only she had asked him, just once, 'Let me come with you.' But she hadn't, and now she wouldn't, which meant she'd never see an alien world.

Instead, her dead eyes closed on the aliens who'd come to hers.

PART TWO
World War Three

PART TWO
World War Three

Monday 6 March 2006, Clancy's, Jordan Road
Mickey Smith sat in the dark, leaning against a pile of car tyres, and he tried not to cry. He'd only started working at Clancy's mechanics a couple of months ago, but he'd already been given a set of keys. After running away from the police surrounding the TARDIS, he'd snuck out of the Powell Estate and come here to hide. He knew he'd need to go home at some point but, right now, he just wanted some peace. The last few hours had been overwhelming. The spaceship, his windows exploding, Big Ben, Jackie seeing inside the TARDIS.

And Rose. Rose and the Doctor. Rose and the Doctor standing next to each other, finishing each other's sentences, perfectly in sync.

Mickey Smith had never felt more alone. He sat in the dark and he tried so so hard not to cry.

He clenched his fists together tightly and forced himself to breathe in deeply. He wasn't going to cry.

'Think of something good,' he whispered to himself. 'Remember something, anything good.'

And he remembered. The day before everything changed.

Mickey has his arms around his girlfriend, Rose, and his good friend Jackie and they're in the Green Dragon. The three of them are singing along with the rest of the pub to 'Always Look On The Bright Side Of Life'. They've just won £50 on the bingo and it's the best night ever. Mickey kisses Rose on the cheek and then Jackie on the cheek and she laughs and calls him cheeky and then Bill the landlord is calling time and Mickey is rushing to get them another drink each and then Bill is confiding in Mickey that they're having a lock-in and Mickey, looking back at the Tyler women cackling away, hopes that this night never ends . . .

Mickey sat in the dark remembering that Friday night. He pictured Jackie, most likely sitting alone in her flat.

Good, he thought, after everything she'd put him through.

Then he started to cry because he hated thinking that way. Jackie Tyler had been like a mum to him. A mum and a best friend. It wasn't her fault that

Rose disappeared for a year. She, like him, had been through so much. He wanted to forgive her.

He *needed* to forgive her, if life was ever to get back to normal.

Mickey jumped up and ran out of the garage, the metal door clattering shut behind him. He ran down the road and into the Powell Estate courtyard. He stopped to catch his breath and looked up at 48 Bucknall House.

He frowned. What was that strange blue light shining out of the window? He started to walk towards the stairwell ...

9

Watch Out for Margaret Thatcher!

The Doctor scrabbled at the ID card in agony as the electricity surged into him. He stared, horrified, at his hand – was it starting to glow?

Was he about to regenerate? He thought about how little these eyes had seen compared to his previous incarnations. What a waste; this wasn't his time! The Doctor screamed and finally, with so much effort, he managed to tear the ID card off his jacket. Choking for air, he looked around, horrified and sickened at the death surrounding him. He remembered Mickey's words in the TARDIS: *You look deep enough on the internet or in the history books, and there's his name. Followed by a list of the dead.*

The Doctor ran to the nearest Slitheen and shoved the ID card into the metal collar around his neck. The electricity attacked. The Slitheen started to writhe in agony – as did the second Slitheen as electricity arced out of the collar around his neck.

The Doctor made a mental note to remember that the collars connected the Slitheen somehow. He wondered how many other Slitheen were currently fighting for their lives because of him. He wondered if he should feel guilty.

And then he started to run.

In the Cabinet Room, the Slitheen dropped Indra's lifeless body and screamed in agony. The electricity coursing through her body was causing her to thrash and flail around dangerously.

Rose grabbed Harriet's hand. 'Run.'

Jackie Tyler was sobbing on her kitchen floor. The policeman *thing* had been terrifying enough with its claws raised over her but now it was a monstrous thrashing giant of electricity. She tried to make herself as small as possible as the thing flailed about and deadly sparks bounced around the kitchen. Then, suddenly, the monster turned away from her. Jackie looked up to see Mickey Smith holding the remains of a chair he'd clearly just hit the alien with. There was a pause as the alien thing seemed to consider its next move.

Mickey reached down and grabbed Jackie, pulling her to her feet and shoving her out of the kitchen. He reached into his pocket, grabbed his phone and quickly took a photo of the alien. He'd show it to the Doctor and Rose – they would know what to do. As the alien screamed and lunged at him, he dodged and grabbed Jackie by the arm. They ran.

The Doctor ran out into the Downing Street entrance hallway . Then he stopped as armed guards quickly surrounded him. They must have heard the carnage, he figured.

He raised his hands. 'If you want aliens, you've got them. They're inside Downing Street. Come on!'

Rose and Harriet ran through corridor after corridor and room after room as the alien scrambled after them. Portraits of kings and queens and prime ministers were sent flying as the alien scrambled up the walls to try and catch its prey. Rose was nearly hit by a particularly large painting of Margaret Thatcher as the alien sent it hurtling through the air towards her. That really did make her scream.

Rose had been running a lot recently – it was how her life with the Doctor had begun – but now she was starting to struggle. The alien was unstoppable, it seemed to live to hunt. Harriet was desperately out of breath and Rose was starting to think that this could be the end.

This could be the night that the police told her mum that she wouldn't be coming home.

Their only hope, she thought, was to find the Doctor and get out of Downing Street. So she kept on running.

Sergeant Donal Price had been working at 10 Downing Street for over fifteen years and he had never known a day like today. In his first week, back in '91, he'd been witness to a terrorist mortar attack on the building and, more recently, he'd seen all sorts of shenanigans at the showbiz parties organised by the missing PM. He'd seen minor royals get drunk and he'd seen visiting presidents get drunker. He'd seen a helluva lot, all told. But he'd never known a day like this.

He led his team as they chased after the strange northerner who claimed there were aliens in the building. Normally, he'd have laughed in the man's face for saying this and maybe given him a slap or two for wasting his time but Sergeant Donal Price, like the rest of the world, had watched the spaceship smash through Big Ben and crash down into the Thames. Everything had changed.

Sergeant Price watched as the big-eared bloke kicked open the door to the briefing room. He followed him into the room and stopped.

It was carnage.

Nearly everyone in the room was dead, their skin blackened and burned and crispy. Donal held his breath. He knew from his days in the army what the smell would be like.

'Where have you been?' asked the acting Prime Minister. Green was standing at the front of the room beside General Asquith; they seemed to be the only ones uninjured. 'I called for help. I sounded the alarm. There was this lightning, this kind of electricity, and they all collapsed.'

Sergeant Price looked at the bodies. 'I think they're all dead.' He was aware he was stating the obvious, but he didn't know what else to say.

'That's what I'm saying,' roared Joseph Green. '*He* did it! That man there.' He pointed at the bloke who'd led them here.

'I think you will find the Prime Minister is an alien in disguise.' The man considered for a moment, then grinned. 'That's never going to work, is it?'

Sergeant Price shook his head, raised his gun and pointed it at the northerner.

'Fair enough.' And the northerner ran.

Jackie Tyler followed Mickey into his flat and shuddered. It was a mess. Clothes were strewn all over the place, dirty dishes were piled up next to the sink. Every piece of furniture looked to be covered in at least an inch of dust.

'Oh, Mickey,' she said quietly, her voice so sad.

He shrugged. 'Not like I get any visitors, is it.' He cleared some newspapers off the sofa and Jackie sat down. 'You all right?'

'Yeah,' she replied. 'I mean, it was a bit of a shock. I was just attacked by an alien, Mickey!'

He looked at her, confused. 'Yeah, but you were also attacked by aliens a year ago.'

'What?' Now she looked confused. 'The shop dummies? No, you muppet, that was a gas leak!'

Mickey opened his mouth and then closed it again. Jackie Tyler would believe whatever Jackie Tyler wanted to believe and there was no changing her mind.

He slumped down into his gran's old armchair and they both looked anywhere but at each other.

The Doctor was running. The Doctor was always running but this time he was running away from one of his greatest fears. Angry human beings with guns.

He thought back to Barry. The harmless, terrified pig running for his life only to have his life ended by a terrified little man. How easily a life could just end ...

He kept running. He found himself again in the entrance hallway. If he'd had Rose with him then he could just run out, get back to the TARDIS and find out who these Slitheen were. But he didn't have Rose with him, and he could never leave without her.

He ran over to the wall across from the entrance. He reached it but suddenly found himself surrounded by police as they came swarming in from all directions. The Doctor was trapped. The situation seemed hopeless.

But the Doctor knew otherwise. He remembered the games of hide and seek with Lloyd George's children. He knew what was here. As the alien pretending to be General Asquith approached, the Doctor's fingers worked over the wall behind his back, trying to find ... aha. He found what he was looking for.

'Under the jurisdiction of the Emergency Protocols, I authorise you to execute this man,' barked General Asquith.

The armed police raised their guns, pointing them at the Doctor.

'Well, now, yes, you see, er, the thing is, if I was you, if I was going to execute someone by backing them against the wall, between you and me, little word of advice.' The Doctor grinned, hearing a 'ding' behind him. 'Don't stand them against the lift!'

The lift doors behind him opened and he stepped back. He buzzed his sonic screwdriver and the doors slammed shut.

The Doctor breathed a sigh of relief. He'd escaped the Slitheen and he'd escaped the armed policemen. Twice. The lift came to a stop on the first floor and the doors opened. A Slitheen turned to face him and giggled.

'This really isn't my night,' said the Doctor with a sigh.

Behind the Slitheen, he saw that Rose and Harriet Jones were trapped in a corner. He reached into his jacket pocket and pulled out a cricket ball. He threw it at the Slitheen, who stomped forward automatically to catch it. Rose and Harriet fled past the Slitheen and ran into the next room. As the Slitheen stared at the cricket ball, the Doctor closed the lift doors and the lift began to ascend once more. He knew where Rose was and he knew how to save her.

*

Rose and Harriet ran into the room and closed the door behind them.

'I can't run any more,' said Harriet, with a sob. 'I'm so sorry, Rose. I hate to be a cliché but you run on and save yourself. I'll try to stop the alien.'

'The giant alien with giant claws, you're gonna try and stop it, are you?' Rose smiled at Harriet. 'Hide!'

They looked around the room. It appeared to be some kind of living quarters with a sofa, a drinks cabinet and a large television set.

'The Doctor knows where we are,' hissed Rose as she hid behind the drinks cabinet. 'He'll be coming for us.'

Harriet ducked behind an ornate free-standing window screen. They held their breaths as the door was pushed open and the alien that had been Margaret Blaine entered the room.

She giggled.

Downstairs, in the entrance hallway, Sergeant Donal Price was confused. He asked General Asquith to clarify the orders he'd been given.

Asquith raised his voice. 'I repeat, the upper floors are under quarantine. You will stay where you are. You will disregard all previous instructions. You will take your orders directly from me.'

Donal didn't understand. There were alien terrorists in Downing Street. 'Mr Green, sir. I'm sorry but you've got to come with me. We should evacuate the entire building.'

The Prime Minister took a step closer towards Donal and smiled patronisingly down at him. 'Sergeant, have you read the Emergency Protocols?'

Sergeant Price shook his head.

'Then don't question me,' continued the Prime Minister. 'Seal off Number 10, secure the ground floor, and if the Doctor makes it downstairs – shoot on sight!'

The Prime Minister and General Asquith stepped into the lift. The doors closed and the lift started to ascend. Sergeant Price shook his head; the Prime Minister was heading directly towards the terrorists. Then he turned to his men, knowing that his place wasn't to question orders. 'Well, you heard him. Move out!'

As his men started to move out across the ground floor, Sergeant Price looked at the lift doors. He couldn't help wondering what was really going on tonight.

10

The Hunt

In the lift, Jocrassa Fel-Fotch Passameer-Day Slitheen, wearing the skin of Joseph Green, turned to his brother, Styles Fel-Fotch Passameer-Day Slitheen, who was wearing the skin of General Ronald Asquith. The lift was cramped and uncomfortable. The skinsuits they had to wear were cramped and uncomfortable. Despite this, the two brothers were smiling. They knew that there were at least three humans trapped on the upper floors.

They were going to have some sport.

Their masterplan, so far, had meant they'd only been able to kill a small number of humans in dishonourable, secretive ways, starting with the humans whose skins they were now wearing. Jocrassa had selected Joseph Green as his target because the human was the physically largest member of this human government and therefore his skin would be the least constricting. He had stalked Green for weeks, learning the human's daily routine. Then, one day, he had waited until the man had been driving home at night and stepped out in front of him. Green had nearly crashed his car into Jocrassa, barely braking in time.

The human had got out of his car and approached Jocrassa, mistaking him for a man in a costume and muttering something about a fancy-dress party. Jocrassa had sighed and slaughtered him on the spot. He'd then lived as Joseph Green for nearly a year – a very dull year for Jocrassa Fel-Fotch Passameer-Day Slitheen since Green had no significant other and very few friends. On the plus side, he'd had mildly inconsiderate neighbours; one night, when they'd played music into the early hours, Jocrassa had enjoyed taking them to a nearby forest for a late-night hunt.

Jocrassa considered his brother's strategy. Initially, the plan had been for him to kill and wear the body of General Asquith from the beginning, but the General's international lifestyle meant that there was a much greater risk of someone discovering the truth. He'd then decided on the relatively minor civil servant Oliver Charles. Oliver had been a big man – an important factor – but Jocrassa did sometimes wonder whether Styles had targeted Oliver Charles more for his lavish lifestyle than his size. As Jocrassa had spent the year living alone and working for his constituents, Styles had enjoyed a year full of parties and illicit affairs with rich human beings, many of whom had had the first name 'Sir' or 'Lord'. He hadn't been able to hunt humans, of course, but he had enjoyed hunting other creatures alongside the humans: foxes, deer, flying pests, all had been fair game for Styles Fel-Fotch Passameer-Day Slitheen. The only time he'd had the opportunity to kill a human was when he had hunted and slaughtered a neighbour's dog. Styles had tried to explain to the neighbour that it made no sense for it to be okay to hunt foxes but not dogs. The neighbour had threatened to call the police, so Styles had taken him home for a quick indoor hunt. The man's head now hung on the wall in the study, next to his dog's.

Jocrassa turned to Styles. 'I meant to ask, how's the wife?'

Styles chortled, 'I'm afraid she discovered my little dalliances with Danny and Janet and she rather lost her head about the whole affair.'

'A good hunt?' asked Jocrassa.

Styles reached into one of his trouser pockets and took out a blood-splattered ginger cream biscuit. He popped into his mouth. 'It was over in seconds,' he replied sadly.

Both Jocrassa and Styles had missed the hunt more than anything else over the last year. Now, as the lift reached the second floor, Styles grinned at his brother. 'Let the sport begin.'

Then, he released more gas and the lift was filled with a beautiful pungent aroma not dissimilar to the human food of fried eggs.

'I'm getting poisoned by the gas exchange,' Jocrassa complained. 'I need to be naked.'

'Rejoice in it. Your body is magnificent!'

Jocrassa and Styles both reached up to their foreheads and unzipped. They would hunt together in their true forms.

The lift pinged and the doors opened.

Rose Tyler, hiding behind the drinks cabinet, was holding her breath as the alien slowly walked into the room. She suspected that the creature was being deliberately slow because it enjoyed the hunt.

'Little human children, where are you?' the alien asked ever-so-sweetly. 'Sweet little humey-kins, come to me. Let me kiss you better. Kiss you with my big, green lips.'

Rose realised, with a chill, that the alien was getting closer to her. She peeked out and saw that it was looking away from her, and she quickly, silently, crawled over to the window so she could hide behind the curtain.

She almost wanted to laugh. She was playing hide-and-seek, in 10 Downing Street, with an alien.

But she had seen what the alien had done to Indra Ganesh so she knew just how deadly this particular game was.

She held her breath as the alien continued to stalk the room, praying that the Doctor would find them soon.

The Doctor inched along a corridor. He knew he was close to the room that Rose and Harriet had run into. He just hoped they were still in there. The Doctor had been to 10 Downing Street a few times in his 900 years, and it always surprised him just how big it was. It wasn't quite TARDIS levels of big but there were still far more rooms than you'd expect.

Suddenly, he heard two voices. Two Slitheen. He saw them. Naked, walking towards him. He ducked into a room and they walked past, not seeing him.

'It does us good to hunt. Purifies the blood,' said one.

'We'll keep this floor quarantined as our last hunting ground before the final phase,' the other replied.

They opened the door to a room at the end of the corridor and went inside.

The Doctor realised, with absolute horror, that it was the room he had helped Rose and Harriet escape into. They would be trapped in there with the Slitheen.

He had to do something.

Mickey was watching television. Tom Hitchinson was standing outside 10 Downing Street. The reporter had been stood there all day, and his face was starting to show it.

'And there's still no word from inside Downing Street, though we are getting even more new arrivals,' he said.

Mickey watched as cars arrived and people exited them.

'That's Group Captain Tennant James of the RAF, though why he's been summoned we've no idea. And that's Ewan McAllister, Deputy Secretary for the Scottish Parliament. And this is most unusual – I'm told that is Sylvia Dillane, Chairman of the North Sea Boating Club. Quite what connects these people, we have no idea.'

Mickey stared at the screen.

'Jackie,' he called through to the kitchen where Rose's mum had taken it upon herself to do the washing up. 'That policeman who attacked you – big guy, wasn't he?'

Jackie came through, drying a mug. She had soap suds in her hair. 'Oh, yeah, he looked like one of those old wrestlers, do you remember? Oh, you'll be too young. My old dad he used to love it. Every Saturday night, it was. ITV. Eamonn Andrews, that's who—'

'Jackie!' Mickey interrupted her and pointed at the screen. 'They're saying these people have been summoned to Downing Street, yeah? But they're not like big, high-up people. Look at them! Can you see a connection?'

Jackie stared at the screen. 'Oh, I see what you mean. They're all, well, big. Not that I'm judging.'

Mickey waited for her to make the connection. It took nearly a full minute and then she gasped.

'You mean they could all have aliens inside them?'

Mickey nodded grimly and tried to call Rose again.

Rose was starting to wish she hadn't switched off her phone. There were now three aliens in the room with her and Harriet, and she realised that this could very much be the end. Should she risk switching her phone back on to try and call the police? But then she'd just be bringing more people to Downing Street to be killed like Indra.

'Happy hunting?' asked one of the aliens who had just entered the room.

'It's wonderful,' replied the alien who had been Margaret Blaine. 'The more you prolong it, the more they stink.'

Rose had been right: the aliens enjoyed hunting.

'Sweat and fear,' said one of the aliens, giggling.

Rose could hear them softly and slowly walking around the room.

'I can smell an old girl,' said one. 'Stale bird and brittle bones.'

Rose hoped Harriet Jones wasn't too scared. She really liked her.

'And a ripe youngster, all hormones and adrenalin. Fresh enough to bend before she snaps.'

Rose realised with horror that the voice describing her was close. Too close. Too late, she saw the shadow of a claw rise above her.

Then it tore down the curtain, revealing her hiding place.

Rose screamed. The alien towered over her, ready

to strike. Tears pouring down her face, Rose looked up. She wouldn't close her eyes.

'No!' screamed a voice. Rose turned to see Harriet jumping out from behind the window screen. 'Take me first! Take me!'

The three aliens paused and then started to giggle. Rose despised them for mocking Harriet's bravery.

Suddenly, the door burst open, and the Doctor pounced in. He was carrying a fire extinguisher. He sprayed foam at the two aliens nearest to him. They shrieked, unable to see. The alien nearest to Rose turned to see what was happening and Rose, using the torn curtain, yanked down the rest of the heavy curtain rail. It smashed down on the alien's big green head.

'Out with me,' yelled the Doctor.

Rose didn't need telling twice. She grabbed Harriet's hand and ran over to the Doctor. They stood behind him as he sprayed the aliens again with the fire extinguisher and then he turned and shooed them away.

The three of them ran down the corridor.

'We need to head to the Cabinet Room,' said the Doctor.

'The Emergency Protocols are in there. They give instructions for aliens,' Harriet Jones replied.

'Sorry, I did say earlier. I'm Harriet Jones, MP for Flydale North.'

'I remember,' the Doctor said, suddenly laughing. 'Harriet Jones, I like you.'

'I think I like you too,' Harriet Jones replied.

The three of them ran through rooms and corridors, hearing the screeching aliens chasing after them and getting closer. Rose had so many questions, but she knew they would have to wait.

They ran and they ran until they reached the Cabinet Room. The Doctor led them inside. He closed the door but it was pushed open immediately. The three aliens stood in the doorway and Rose realised that, once again, they were trapped.

She knew this time, though, that they had the Doctor with them. She took Harriet's hand and gave it a squeeze. Everything was going to be okay. She took a deep breath and waited to see what would happen.

The Doctor picked up a heavy glass decanter from one of the side tables and pointed his sonic screwdriver at it.

'One more move and my sonic device will triplicate the flammability of this alcohol. Whoof, we all go up. So back off.'

The three aliens backed off.

Still holding the sonic screwdriver and the decanter, the Doctor continued. 'Right then. Question time. Who exactly are the Slitheen?'

Rose realised that must be what the aliens were called.

Next to her, Harriet piped up, helpfully. 'They're aliens.'

Rose heard the Doctor fail to hide the irritation in his voice. 'Yes. I got that, thanks.'

One of the Slitheen looked at the Doctor. Or rather at the sonic screwdriver. 'Who are you, if not human?'

'Who's not human?' asked Harriet.

'He's not human,' replied Rose.

'He's not human?' asked Harriet, staring at the Doctor.

Rose was about to tell her about how the Doctor was the last of the Time Lords when the last of the Time Lords turned around and stared at them both.

'Can I have a bit of hush?'

Rose and Harriet apologised.

The Doctor turned back to face the Slitheen. 'So, what's the plan?'

Harriet suddenly piped up again. 'But he's got a northern accent.' She pointed at the Doctor.

Rose grinned. She'd once said the very same thing. She gave Harriet the answer that the Doctor had given her. 'Lots of planets have a north.'

'I said hush,' said the Doctor. 'Speaking of north, you've got a spaceship hidden in the North Sea. It's transmitting a signal. You've murdered your way to the top of government. What for, invasion?'

One of the Slitheen giggled. 'Why would we invade this godforsaken rock?'

'Then something's brought the Slitheen race here,' said the Doctor. 'What is it?'

This time the Slitheen didn't giggle. In fact, it sounded offended, thought Rose.

'The Slitheen race? Slitheen is not our species. Slitheen is our surname. Jocrassa Fel-Fotch Passameer-Day-Slitheen at your service.'

'So you're a family,' said the Doctor.

'A family business,' replied the Slitheen proudly.

'Then you're out to make a profit. How can you do that on a godforsaken rock?'

There was a pause and then one of the Slitheen took a step forward. 'Ah, excuse me? Your device will do what – triplicate the flammability?'

The Doctor shrugged, looking at the sonic screwdriver. 'Is that what I said?'

'You're making it up.'

Rose tried not to panic. It was clear that the Slitheen were working out that they could actually just simply enter the room and kill them. The Doctor passed the decanter back towards Harriet.

'Ah, well. Nice try. Harriet, have a drink. I think you're going to need it.'

Harriet shook her head. 'You pass it to the left first.'

Rose had no idea what Harriet was talking about, but she took the decanter as the Doctor instead handed it back towards her. She stared at the Slitheen as they started to move towards the doorway.

'Now we can end this hunt with a slaughter,' one of them announced as the other two giggled.

The Doctor just grinned at them. 'Fascinating history, Downing Street. Two thousand years ago, this was marshland. 1730, it was occupied by a Mr Chicken. He was a nice man. 1796, this was the Cabinet Room. If the Cabinet's in session and in danger, these are about the four safest walls in the whole of Great Britain. End of lesson.'

As Rose, Harriet and the three Slitheen watched, the Doctor lifted a panel next to the door and pressed a button. Metal shutters instantly crashed shut across each window and door. The Slitheen were locked outside the room.

Rose and Harriet both breathed a sigh of relief. The Doctor turned to face them.

'Installed in 1991,' he explained, with a grin. 'Three inches of steel lining every single wall. They'll never get in.'

'And how do we get out?' asked Rose.

The Doctor's face fell. 'Ah.'

Downstairs, in the staff toilet, Sergeant Donal Price was making a phone call. His job was and always had been to not question orders. But he knew something was very wrong in Downing Street. The alien experts had all been killed. The Prime Minister was missing. Even Indra Ganesh seemed to have vanished.

'Hello?' Donal breathed a sigh of relief at the sound of Sergeant Helen Zbrigniev's voice.

'Helen, it's Donal,' he replied. 'Are you still in Brighton with the rest of the Cabinet?'

'Yeah,' she replied. 'Is it true, mate? Is it aliens?'

'Yeah, looks like it.' He took a deep breath. 'Is ... is everything, I don't know, is everything normal there?'

He heard Helen clear her throat. 'Well,' she paused before continuing. 'It's a bit odd. So, we've been told there's been an outbreak of some kind of swine flu here in the hotel.'

'Oh,' replied Donal.

'Oh, indeed. So, the members of the Cabinet, they've all been isolated in their rooms. Only, I've not heard from any of them for at least a couple of hours. Not since the doctor did his rounds.'

'He visited them in their rooms?'

'Yeah,' she replied. 'And he immediately insisted that they went into quarantine.'

'Makes sense,' Donal replied. His voice, though, made it very clear he didn't trust the situation.

He heard Helen lower her voice to a whisper. 'But, thing is, not one of them has phoned out for room service or anything.'

Donal knew Helen. He knew she'd obey her orders to the letter; she was a good soldier. And he knew that something was very, very wrong.

'Thanks, Helen,' he said. 'Keep me posted. I think it's going to be a long night.'

'Tell me about it!' He heard her laugh. 'Oh, and Donal, mate, you should see the doctor they sent us. The man's the size of a house!'

11

The Locked Room Mystery

Mickey Smith leaned back in his chair.

'I hate this,' he said, pointing at the TV where Tom Hitchinson was still standing outside 10 Downing Street. 'She's trapped in there. And we're trapped in here.'

He turned to see Jackie Tyler picking up a pile of clothes. 'I'll take this lot down the laundrette tomorrow.'

'You don't need to,' Mickey replied.

Jackie looked at him. 'I think I do.'

He smiled at her. 'I've missed you, Jacks.'

'Since my Pete died, you're the only one who ever calls me that.' Her eyes suddenly filled with tears. 'I'm so sorry, Mickey. I was just so scared and confused and I didn't know. You understand? I didn't know where she was, and you'd seen her, and I hadn't seen her, so it made sense that it was you even though I hated thinking it was you and ...'

He stood up and quickly went over to her. He paused. He wanted to hug her, but were they there yet? So he stood there, arms outstretched, frozen.

'Oh, just give me a hug, you total lemon,' she said, bursting into tears.

Mickey quickly wrapped her up in his arms.

'Do you hate me?' she asked, sobbing into his chest.

'Never could,' he replied. 'You've been like my mum and my best mate all these years. Love you, Jacks.'

And with that, the two friends realised and hoped that perhaps everything could be okay.

He stepped back and wiped the tears from his eyes. 'Right, I'll go make us a cuppa.'

Jackie smiled. 'Got anything stronger?'

He laughed. 'No chance. I've seen you when you've had a few. This ain't time for a conga.' He left the room, heading through to his now spotless kitchen.

'We've got to tell someone,' Jackie called after him.

'Who do we trust?' Mickey called back. 'For all we know, they've all got big bog monsters inside of them. I mean, this is what he does, Jacks, that Doctor bloke. Everywhere he goes, death and destruction, and he's got Rose in the middle of it.'

Jackie followed him through to the kitchen, looking for a bin bag for the laundry. 'Has he got a great big green thing inside him, then?' she asked as she started rooting through drawers.

'I wouldn't put it past him,' Mickey replied as he filled the kettle. 'But like it or not, he's the only person who knows how to fight these things.'

He plugged the kettle in and switched it on. Jackie found some bin bags under the kitchen sink and started to fill one with Mickey's laundry. Then she stopped.

'I thought I was going to die,' she whispered, close to tears again.

He gave her a goofy grin. 'Come on, yeah? If anyone's going to cry, it's going to be me.' He gave her another hug. 'Now, you're safe in my flat, Jacks. No one's going to look for you here, especially since you hate me so much.'

She chuckled. 'You saved my life. God, that's embarrassing.'

He grinned back at her. 'You're telling me.'

Sergeant Donal Price really had no idea what was going on now. He was still thinking about his phone call with Helen in Brighton. Why did he feel like they were all being isolated from each other? He was considering contacting the UN directly with his concerns when one of his men called him to the entrance hallway. He arrived to find the man, Murphy, arguing with three new arrivals.

'I've tried to explain to them, sir,' Murphy said to Donal. 'But they won't leave.'

Donal dismissed Murphy and tried to take control of the situation. A particularly large man introduced himself as Group Captain Tennant James of the RAF as he gave Sergeant Price a bone-crushing handshake. He then introduced his companions as Ewan McAllister from the Scottish Parliament and Sylvia Dillane, Chairman of the North Sea Boating Club. The Group Captain insisted that they'd been invited to Downing Street by the Prime Minister.

'But we're securing the building,' Donal tried to explain. 'We've never had a situation like this; you must have seen the news!'

The Group Captain put a huge, heavy hand on Donal's shoulder. Donal tried not to recoil from the man's breath. McAllister and Dillane moved in closer. The Group Captain smiled down at Donal. 'You should probably just do as you're told, shouldn't you?'

'Orders are orders,' said Syliva Dillane.

Ewan McAllister gave a high-pitched giggle.

'I'll . . . I'll take you through to one of the waiting rooms,' said Donal.

The Group Captain leaned down. 'Good boy.'

'Group Captain!' a voice called out from the stairs. They turned to see Margaret Blaine coming down the stairs, smiling and waving. 'Delighted you could make it.'

The Group Captain and his companions headed over to the stairs to join Margaret. As they did, Ewan McAllister suddenly farted and giggled.

'That's the spirit,' said Margaret happily.

Sergeant Donal Price just stared and wondered if he was having some kind of breakdown.

'Ah, Sergeant,' a voice called. He turned to see General Asquith striding towards him. 'Now that the Doctor's been neutralised, the upper levels are out of bounds to everyone.'

Donal was this close to screaming out in frustration. Margaret Blaine had literally just taken three people – including the chairman of the North Sea Boating Club – upstairs. He clenched his fists.

'Then who are they?' he asked calmly as he indicated the stairs.

'Need to know, Sergeant, need to know,' replied Asquith, with a patronising tone. 'I want you to liaise with Communications. The acting Prime Minister will be making a public address. He will speak to the nations of the world.'

Asquith strode off, heading up the stairs.

Constable Murphy joined him. 'Everything all right, sir?'

Sergeant Donal Price shook his head. 'No, Murphy. No. There is something very, very wrong happening here.'

'The ambulances have arrived to collect the stiffs,' said Murphy, indicating the briefing room. Donal remembered the carnage he'd seen in there.

'Okay, but the bodies need to be taken out the back, away from the reporters.' Donal didn't need to explain but he chose to. 'People are scared, Neil. People in here, people out there, people watching it all on TV. Scared people can do stupid things so let's not scare them even more with a bunch of bodies, yeah?'

Constable Murphy nodded.

'And treat them with respect, Constable,' Donal added. 'They were people, just like us.'

Right, he thought, as Murphy sloped away. *I'd better liaise with Communications. Orders are orders.*

Upstairs, the Slitheen wearing Margaret Blaine's skin stood outside the toilets holding a coat hanger.

Blon Fel-Fotch Passameer-Day Slitheen was the youngest of the Slitheen family. Ever since the day she had hatched, she had had to fight – not only for respect but just for the chance to live. From inside the toilets, one of her brothers was calling out to her.

'I just went from room to room and picked them off one by one.' Phipps Fel-Fotch Passameer-Day Slitheen was a couple of lunar cycles older than Blon, and she'd always despised him. When they were young hatchlings, he had often tried to push her into a deadly pit of venom grubs and now she had to stand and listen to him boast about his adventures in Brighton. 'Then I hopped on the train back to London. Honestly, it was almost too easy.' Phipps smiled politely as he left the toilets and handed her his skinsuit. 'Oh look! There's me having to kill the rest of the Government's leaders all by myself and here's you, holding a coat hanger.' He chuckled as he stomped off down the corridor.

Blon kept smiling. She knew that her time was coming. She had chosen Margaret Blaine as her victim because the family needed someone in the British intelligence services. Margaret had, like Joseph Green, been something of a loner so it had actually been quite easy to replace her but, in many ways, Blon had had the hardest job. People who worked for the intelligence services, like MI5, were constantly being watched by their colleagues and employers to check that they hadn't been secretly recruited by another country. Blon had managed to stay successfully undercover for an entire year. That meant, though, that she'd gone an entire year without killing and she had missed it. Tonight, after slaughtering both the Prime Minister and Indra Ganesh, she was on a high. She had felt the life leave their bodies and she needed more. Before the end of everything, she would find more humans to hunt. She would prove to Phipps that she was every bit the Slitheen that he was.

But for now, Blon Fel-Fotch Passameer-Day Slitheen was standing outside the toilets holding a coat hanger. Mulhol Fel-Fotch Passameer-Day Slitheen came out from the toilets and hung his Tennant James skinsuit on the coat hanger.

'Now, if you'd like to head down to the end of the corridor,' said Blon, 'it's first on the left.'

Her brother nodded. 'Thank you,' he growled as he stomped off down the corridor.

Jocrassa, still wearing his Joseph Green skinsuit, stepped out of the lift and joined his sister.

'Is that all of us?'

'All except Sip Fel-Fotch,' she replied as she straightened out the Tennant James skinsuit. 'He's found a hunt of his own.'

She started to giggle.

Sip Fel-Fotch Passameer-Day Slitheen looked at himself in the mirror as he readjusted his skinsuit. Six months before, Terence Strickland had been an easy slaughter but, as his victim had been popular with his workmates, Sip had had to work hard to ensure nobody suspected he was anything other than the gentle giant of a human being that they all loved. It had been four months since his last kill – a homeless man he'd taken to an abandoned industrial estate – and he was ravenous for the hunt. Earlier that evening he'd been so close to slaughtering his young policeman colleague. Then those two other human idiots had joined them. He could easily have ended all three of their miserable little lives with one swipe of his claw but that would have put the Slitheen masterplan in jeopardy. Once he had dealt with Mrs Tyler, perhaps he'd have time to join his colleagues in the pub. Of course, he thought to himself, it was far too late for Jackie

Tyler to be any kind of threat to the Slitheen. He just really wanted to hear her final screams. Then, job done, he could head to the pub. He pictured himself barricading the doors so that there'd be no escape. Oh, the terror, the fear, the panic of the humans in the pub as he revealed his true naked form. He would savour the slaughter. He would take as long as he wanted. Or at least, Sip thought, as long it took for the Slitheen plan to reach fruition.

Until then, he had two targets here on the Powell Estate to eliminate. The woman was weak and would be an easy kill. The young human male who had rescued her would be more of a challenge. Sip enjoyed a challenge. He liked it best when they still had hope. When they still had hope, he could crush it along with their skulls.

He left the Tylers' flat and slowly started to stalk the corridors of the Powell Estate. He had their scent, and he would use it to find them ...

'You must never pass the port across the table or back on itself.' Harriet was explaining to Rose why port had to be passed to the left. 'Historically, I think, it's so that you could keep your sword arm free.'

Suddenly, Harriet found herself laughing. She thought back to her train journey, that morning, when she'd had no idea what the day was going to become.

'Are you all right?' Rose asked her.

She was a kind girl, Harriet thought. The Doctor was kind too. They were kind people.

'I'm just, well, a little exhausted. I'll be fine.'

The Doctor rejoined them. He had carried the body of Indra Ganesh into the large cupboard with the Prime Minister's body.

'Sleep well, Indra Ganesh,' he muttered before closing the door. 'Right, what have we got? Any terminals, anything?'

'No,' Rose replied. 'This place is antique. What I don't get is, when they killed the Prime Minister, why didn't they use him as a disguise?'

Harriet was about to reply but the Doctor got there first. 'He's too slim. They're big old beasts. They need to fit inside big humans.'

'But the Slitheen are about eight feet,' Rose pointed out. 'How do they fit inside?'

The Doctor realised what the Slitheen collars were for. 'That's the device around their necks! Compression field. Literally shrinks them down a bit. That's why there's all that gas. It's a big exchange.'

Harriet watched the two of them. It was like watching a tennis match – back and forth, back and forth. She sat down and started to go through the Emergency Protocols once more.

'Wish I had a compression field,' said Rose with a grin. 'I could fit a size smaller.'

Harriet couldn't believe what she had just heard. 'Excuse me, people are dead! This is not the time for making jokes.'

Rose looked a little ashamed. 'Sorry,' she said. 'You get used to this stuff when you're friends with him.'

'Well, that's a strange friendship,' Harriet replied.

The Doctor spun round to look at her. 'Harriet Jones. I've heard that name before. Harriet Jones. You're not famous for anything, are you?'

She felt as if he was staring into her soul and it scared her. 'Lifelong backbencher, I'm afraid, and a fat lot of use I'm being now.' She sat back in her chair. 'The Protocols are redundant. They list the people who could help and they're all dead downstairs.'

Rose sat down next to her and started to look through the red folder. 'Hasn't it got, like, defence codes and things? Couldn't we just launch a nuclear bomb at them?'

Harriet stared at her. 'You're a very violent young woman.'

'I'm serious. We could.'

'Well, there's nothing like that in here,' Harriet explained. 'Nuclear strikes do need a release code, yes, but it's kept secret by the United Nations.'

The Doctor rushed over to join them. 'Say that again.'

Harriet looked up at him. 'What, about the codes?'

'Anything. All of it.'

'Well,' said Harriet. 'The British Isles can't gain access to atomic weapons without a Special Resolution from the UN.'

Rose snorted. 'Like that's ever stopped them.'

'Exactly,' said Harriet. 'Given our past record – and I voted against that, thank you very much – the codes have been taken out of the Government's hands and given to the UN. Is it important?'

'Everything's important,' the Doctor replied.

'If we only knew what the Slitheen wanted.' Harriet laughed. 'Listen to me. I'm saying Slitheen as if it's normal.'

She watched as Rose took her phone out of her pocket and switched it on.

The Doctor looked at Harriet. 'Well, they're just one family, so it's not an invasion. They don't want

Slitheen World. They're out to make money. That means they want to use something. Something here on Earth. Some kind of asset.'

'Like what, gold? Oil? Water?' said Harriet.

'You're very good at this,' said the Doctor.

Harriet smiled. There was something about this Doctor. Even though he was younger than her – well, she assumed he was – the Doctor reminded her of her father. She remembered the day she had taken her old dad to the pub to tell him what she wanted to do with her life. She'd sat him down with a pint of his favourite bitter and told him that she wanted to get into politics.

He had looked surprised at first. She knew he'd always imagined that she would marry Richard Morris from the undertakers, become a housewife and a mother. She also knew that he would never fully understand why a woman would want to work in politics or indeed at all. But her father had just taken her hand, smiled and said, 'I am very proud of you for doing what you want to do and not what I want you to do.'

Rose's phone beeped. And beeped again. And again, and again. She pulled a face. 'Yeah, quite a few missed calls from Mickey and my mum.'

'But we're sealed off,' said Harriet. She had tried to call her mother earlier but there was no signal.

'He zapped it,' said Rose. 'Super phone.'

Harriet jumped to her feet. 'Then we can phone for help! You must have contacts.'

The Doctor turned to face her. 'Dead, downstairs, yeah. Friend of mine, actually. Muriel Frost.' The Doctor's face showed no sadness but, to Harriet, it was clearly a mask. 'She was brilliant, actually.' Harriet desperately wanted to hug him but Rose's phone beeped again and the Doctor snarled, 'Oh, tell your stupid boyfriend we're busy!'

Harriet saw that the Doctor instantly regretted snapping at Rose but Rose, it seemed, hadn't even noticed. She was just holding up her phone. On it was a picture sent by Mickey Smith. A blurry pixellated picture of a Slitheen.

Rose smirked. 'Yeah, he's not so stupid after all.'

Mickey Smith and Jackie Tyler had devised a plan.

Mickey knew about the Doctor's connection with UNIT. He would find a way to contact them and let them know that the Doctor was in Downing Street. UNIT would then rescue him and Rose. Sorted.

Jackie was more worried about the alien that was hunting her. What if it hurt or killed any of their neighbours? Mickey pointed out that the aliens wanted everyone watching Downing Street. They wouldn't want to distract anyone with a massacre on the Powell Estate. There wasn't much they could do other than sit and wait for help.

Jackie looked out through the space where Mickey's bedroom window had been. 'You wanna get these boarded up properly,' she murmured. 'There's an owl out there sometimes, you can hear him. The last thing you want is an owl in your bedroom.'

Jackie was sure she could see the tiniest hint of a ribbon of light in the dark night sky. She smiled, thinking of Molly Steer down on the ground floor. She knew that Molly always got up to watch the sunrise and she imagined her, down there, pottering around in her kitchen. Lovely Molly, just living her life, doing her thing.

'What do they want?' she asked Mickey. 'These aliens. Why can't they just leave us alone?'

'Do you mean the big green ones or the Doctor?'

She smiled weakly. Both of them knew what she meant.

Mickey's phone started to ring. He picked it up. 'Rose!'

Jackie tried to grab the phone. 'What's she saying? Is she safe?' she wailed.

Mickey turned to her. 'I don't know, Jacks, I can't hear her if a certain someone keeps shouting in my ear.'

Jackie tried to calm down. Rose was phoning Mickey, which meant Rose was safe. That was the main thing.

Jackie had a sudden urge to make some more tea.

'So what happened?' Rose asked Mickey urgently. 'Where was it?'

'It had gone after Jackie,' he replied. 'It was in your kitchen.'

Rose felt her stomach lurch. 'It went after my mum?'

She heard her mum cry out. 'I could've died!'

She felt Harriet's hand take hers. Rose tried not to sound scared. Mickey and her mum had always needed her to be the strong one. 'Is Mum all right, though? Don't put her on, just tell me.'

Before Mickey could answer, the Doctor had grabbed her phone off her. She glared at him.

'Is that Ricky? Don't talk, just shut up and go to your computer.'

*

Mickey fumed. 'It's Mickey. And why should I?'

And then Mickey heard what might have been the greatest thing he'd ever heard in his life. 'Mickey the Idiot, I might just choke before I finish this sentence but, I need you.'

There was a pause. Mickey grinned. 'Say that again, Doc.'

12

Buffalo Stance

Jackie Tyler brought two mugs of tea through to Mickey's bedroom. He was holding his phone and loading up a website on his computer.

'What's that, then?' she asked, nodding at the screen.

'UNIT,' he replied. 'Unified Intelligence Taskforce. The Doc used to work for them.'

'It's Doctor,' said the Doctor on the phone.

'It's Mickey,' replied Mickey. 'It says "password".'

'I've attached Rose's phone to the speaker in here so you should be able to hear all of us,' said the Doctor. 'Say again.'

'It's asking for the password,' Mickey replied.

'Buffalo. Two Fs, one L.'

As Mickey typed in the password, Jackie sipped her tea. 'So what's that website?'

'All the secret information known to mankind,' said Mickey as the screen changed. He stared in awe. The website was far more advanced than anything he'd ever seen before. 'See, they've known about aliens for years. They just kept us in the dark.'

The Doctor chuckled. 'Mickey, you were born in the dark.'

Mickey was about to ask him again what his problem was when he heard Rose.

'Oh, leave him alone,' she said.

Mickey smiled. 'Thank you. Password again.'

'Just repeat it every time,' the Doctor replied.

Mickey handed his phone to Jackie so he could concentrate on typing.

Buffalo. Buffalo. Buffalo.

In Downing Street, Harriet was pouring each of them a glass of port. She wasn't sure whether Rose was old enough to drink or not, but she wasn't going to say anything.

'Big Ben,' said the Doctor to Rose. 'Why did the Slitheen go and hit Big Ben?'

Harriet looked up from the decanter of port. 'You said to gather the experts, to kill them.'

'Who's that, then?' asked a voice from the speaker.

'Harriet Jones, MP, Flydale North,' Harriet replied. 'You must be Rose's mother.'

'Yes, I am,' said the voice. 'You'd better be looking after her.'

Harriet grinned at Rose. 'Oh, I think she's the one looking after us.'

'Right, right,' said the Doctor. 'To gather the experts and kill them. That lot would've gathered for a weather balloon. You don't need to crash land in the middle of London.'

Rose had started to walk around the desk. 'The Slitheen are hiding, but then they put the entire planet on red alert. What would they do that for?'

Jackie's voice sounded from the speaker. 'Oh, listen to her.'

Harriet winced, seeing the look of disappointment on Rose's face as her mother dismissed her. Mothers, she knew from personal experience, could be cruel without meaning to be. She took a glass of port over to Rose and then one to the Doctor.

'At least I'm trying,' said Rose.

'Well, I've got a question, if you don't mind,' said Jackie Tyler with a tone that suggested she was going to ask it regardless. 'Since that man walked into our lives, I have been attacked in the streets. I have had creatures from the pits of hell in my own living room, and my daughter disappear off the face of the Earth.'

Rose was so quiet as she replied. 'I told you what happened.'

Jackie raised her voice. 'I'm talking to him. Cos I've seen this life of yours, Doctor, and maybe you get off on it, and maybe you think it's all clever and smart, but you tell me, just answer me this. Is my daughter safe?'

'I'm fine,' said Rose.

Harriet thought about all the horror she'd witnessed that night. Rose wasn't fine.

'Is she safe?' asked Jackie. 'Will she always be safe? Can you promise me that?'

The Doctor just stared down at his hands. Harriet wondered why they were shaking.

'Well, what's the answer?' demanded Jackie.

Harriet could see that the Doctor had no answer. She tried to think of something to say in his place, but then the young man's voice sounded over the speaker.

'We're in.'

Mickey was looking at a map of the world on the UNIT website. He heard Jackie pacing behind him as the Doctor instructed him on what to do next.

'Now then, on the left at the top, there's a tab, an icon. Little concentric circles. Click on that.'

Mickey clicked on it. The screen changed to a visualisation of some kind of energy reading accompanied by the sound of a repeated set of beeps. This was all far beyond Mickey's understanding. 'What is it?'

'The Slitheen have got a spaceship in the North Sea and it's transmitting that signal. Now hush, let me work out what it's saying.'

Jackie sat back down next to him. 'He'll have to answer me one day.'

Mickey felt for her, of course he did. Everything she had said was true. They all knew Rose wasn't safe but, right now, nobody on the planet was safe and the Doctor needed to do his thing. He put a hand on Jackie's arm and gently shushed her so he could listen.

'It's some sort of message,' said the Doctor.

'What's it say?' asked Rose.

'Don't know, it's on a loop,' said the Doctor. 'Keeps repeating.'

Mickey's doorbell rang.

'Hush,' the Doctor called out.

'That's not me,' said Mickey. He turned to Jackie. 'Go and see who that is.'

'It's three o'clock in the morning,' she replied.

'Well, go and tell them that!'

Jackie left the room in a huff, and Mickey listened as the Doctor spoke to Rose.

'It's beaming out into space. Who's it for?'

Despite himself, Mickey was trying to think of an answer. Could there be more Slitheen out there in space, waiting for a signal to invade?

Suddenly, he heard a scream. He turned as Jackie came running back into his bedroom.

'I looked through the little peephole! It's him,' she cried out. 'It's the thing, it's the Slickeen!'

'They've found us,' said Mickey.

He grabbed Jackie's hand.

In the Cabinet Room, Rose could feel the panic rising inside of her. Harriet quickly took her hand again.

'Mickey,' said the Doctor. 'I need that signal.'

Rose pulled free from Harriet and, full of so much rage, shoved the Doctor to one side. Her mind was overwhelmed with images as she imagined her mum and Mickey being killed like Indra. She yelled into the phone. 'Never mind the signal, get out! Mum! Just get out! Get out!'

There was a second of silence. Mickey's voice sounded again. 'We can't. It's by the front door.'

Rose turned to stare at the Doctor. She didn't hate him, she could never hate him, but why wasn't he doing anything? She choked back a sob. She didn't know want to say, she didn't know what to do. Her mind was trying to picture the scene in Mickey's flat. Was he protecting her mum? Was her mum protecting him? What were they wearing? She couldn't remember what they'd been wearing. She started to feel dizzy and held on to the desk as she tried to force words out.

Then it was Harriet Jones who was raging at the Doctor. 'There's got to be some way of stopping them! You're supposed to be the expert, think of something!'

'I'm trying,' the Doctor snarled back at her. And Rose realised that he was. His impossible alien nine-hundred-year-old mind was trying to work out what to do.

'I'll take it on, Jackie,' Mickey was saying. 'You just run. Don't look back. Just run.'

Rose wanted to cry, hearing Mickey trying to save her mum. She moved to the Doctor's side and took his hands in hers. She looked at him, their eyes meeting. 'That's my mother.'

Galvanised, the Doctor jumped up onto the desk. 'Right, if we're going to find their weakness, we need to find out where they're from. Which planet. So, judging by their basic shape, that narrows it down to

5,000 planets within travelling distance. What else do we know about them? Information!'

'They're green,' said Rose.

'Yep, narrows it down.'

'Good sense of smell.'

'Narrows it down.'

'They can smell adrenalin.'

'Narrows it down.'

Harriet joined in. 'The pig technology.'

'Narrows it down.'

Rose tried to think of anything else.

Mickey's voice sounded over the speaker. 'It's getting in!'

Rose was desperate. 'They ... hunt like it's a ritual.'

The Doctor stomped on the desk. 'Narrows it down!'

'Wait a minute. Did you notice?' said Harriet. 'When they fart, if you'll pardon the word, it doesn't just smell like a fart, if you'll pardon the word, it's something else. What is it? It's more like ...'

'Bad breath!' Rose cried out.

'Calcium decay! Now, that narrows it down!'

Rose could see the Doctor was close. She yelled into her phone. 'We're getting there, Mum!'

Mickey yelled back. 'Too late!'

Rose looked up at the Doctor as he stood on the desk, staring up at the ceiling. 'Calcium phosphate,' he gabbled. 'Organic calcium. Living calcium. Creatures made out of living calcium. What else? What else? Hyphenated surname. Yes! That narrows it down to one planet. Raxacoricofallapatorius!'

Mickey held Jackie behind him as he raised his baseball bat. It might just give them a few extra seconds. He could tell Jackie was terrified – she hadn't said anything in minutes. And whatever the Doctor was saying was useless. 'Oh, yeah, great. We could write 'em a letter.'

Mickey's front door exploded into shards as a giant gnarly foot smashed through it. The Slitheen pushed through the shards and stared down the hallway at them. It threw its human skin at them.

The Doctor's voice shouted down the phone. 'Get into the kitchen!'

Mickey and Jackie ran into the kitchen as the Slitheen stalked towards them. They shut the door, and Mickey quickly rammed a chair up against it.

'Calcium, weakened by the compression field. Acetic acid. Vinegar!' said the Doctor, although Mickey could barely hear him as the Slitheen started to punch and tear at the kitchen door.

'Just like Hannibal,' called out Harriet Jones.

Mickey looked at Jackie and shrugged.

'Just like Hannibal,' the Doctor replied. 'Mickey, have you got any vinegar?'

'How should I know?'

Outside the kitchen, the Slitheen was starting to shriek as it attacked the door.

'It's your kitchen,' shouted the Doctor.

'Cupboard by the sink,' Rose yelled into the phone. 'Middle shelf!'

Jackie grabbed the phone off Mickey, leaving him to try and hold the chair against the door. 'Oh, give it here. What do you need?'

'Anything with vinegar,' shouted the Doctor.

Jackie grabbed the washing-up bowl and opened the nearest cupboard. She grabbed jars and tins and started to pour them into the bowl. 'Gherkins! Yeah, pickled onions! Pickled eggs!'

Mickey turned to see what Jackie was doing. The chair came loose from under the door handle and the door exploded in. The giant green terrifying Slitheen stood there, and it smiled at them.

Taking its time, it slowly moved into the small kitchen.

Mickey turned to Jackie, who was holding the plastic bowl filled with vinegar, gherkins, onions and eggs. She looked at him. He nodded towards the Slitheen. Jackie shrugged. He nodded again and Jackie understood. She chucked the bowl's contents at the Slitheen, and it stopped moving.

It looked at them. 'For the love of Clom,' it roared.

Mickey Smith would never forget what happened next. First, the Slitheen's skin started to crack under the stinking mixture of onions and vinegar. As its roars became screams, the Slitheen's skin started to try and stretch over the cracks, flaps of skin trying to reform into something solid. But, underneath the skin, bulges were forming as the vinegar seeped into the monster's internal organs, and they started to liquefy. It carried on screaming as compressed gas and dissolved organs started to push through the cracks, and Mickey's kitchen quickly filled with a stench even worse than sprouts. The cracked green skin made one last valiant attempt to hold in the last of the gas but then, with a huge belching fart, the Slitheen exploded. Green and yellow chunks of alien monster shot out and splattered over every wall, ceiling, plate, cup and human being in the room.

Mickey could hear Rose's tinny voice asking if they were okay. He wiped his eyes and picked up his phone. 'It worked.'

Back in the Cabinet Office, Rose, unable to speak, motioned quickly for the Doctor to end the call. He looked at her, confused, but Harriet immediately understood. She rushed over and, keeping her voice jolly, spoke into the phone. 'You two clean yourselves up, we'll call you back in a moment.' She ended the call then rushed back to catch Rose as the young girl collapsed, loudly sobbing with exhausted relief. She held on to her so tightly.

'Hannibal crossed the Alps by dissolving boulders with vinegar,' she whispered in Rose's ear.

Rose smiled up at her. 'Oh. Well, there you go, then.'

Then Rose Tyler took a deep breath, wiped away her tears and stood up. They'd saved her mother and her boyfriend, but they still had to save the planet.

13

The End of the World

Jocrassa Fel-Fotch Passameer-Day Slitheen was sitting in the dark. He'd been sitting in silence for what might have been minutes, hours or years. His brother was dead. He had felt it. Sip Fel-Fotch Passameer-Day Slitheen was gone. The Slitheen family had lost a valued solider and he had lost a dear, beloved brother.

Although, he thought, the profit would now be split seven ways rather than eight, so it wasn't all bad.

He left his office and headed down the corridor. His brother Styles was looking down over the balcony into the entrance hallway.

Styles turned to him. 'He's dead. Sip Fel-Fotch—'

'I felt it. How could that happen?'

'Somebody must have got lucky,' Styles replied.

'That's the last piece of luck anyone on this rock will ever have,' Jocrassa snarled. He looked down over the balcony, watching the ambulance crews removing the bodies of the alien experts. That had been a disappointingly easy mass killing. 'Look at those honourable medics, carrying away their fallen. If only we had time to hunt.'

'Could we make time?' asked Styles.

Jocrassa shook his head. 'It's time for the next phase.' He smiled. 'Soon, every single creature on this planet will die, screaming into the night.'

Molly Steer looked out of her kitchen window and watched the fox in the courtyard. The fox, seeming to sense that he was being observed, stared back at Molly. She gave him a friendly smile, and he returned to hunting down his breakfast.

It was still dark outside but tiny pools of sunlight were just starting to become visible behind the dark clouds.

Molly hobbled back over to her chair and sat down. She looked up at the black-and-white newspaper clipping framed on the wall above the sideboard and raised her mug. Then she switched on her television.

In the Green Dragon, PC Tristan White thanked Bill the landlord again for agreeing to a lock-in and, especially, for letting him, Andi and Emma stay. Bill shrugged. He figured anyone who arrested him for staying open late on the day that aliens came to Earth needed locking up themselves. Didn't all their rules and laws suddenly seem all so very small now they knew there was life out there in the stars? Tristan had agreed and had ordered another three pints. The television set, hanging in the corner of the room, was still showing the same footage of the spaceship crashing through Big Ben. He sat back down with his two workmates, and they all stared up at the screen.

In New York, Trinity Wells, fuelled by endless cups of plain coffee and caffeine pills, continued to report on the events in London. Of course, nothing had actually happened for the last few hours, so she had very little to report. She had spent the last hour giving the life stories of anyone who had been seen entering 10 Downing Street. She'd even puzzled over a picture of Rose and the Doctor. 'And can anyone identify these two? Could they be the aliens themselves disguised as human beings? We don't know either way and it would be wrong to speculate.' Many other news anchors in the States had given up on the story by now, but Trinity's journalistic instincts told her something was going to happen. And it was going to happen soon.

*

In a small flat in Cardiff, Toshiko Sato sat on her bed, hugging herself as she watched the never-ending news. She thought back to her phone call with Jack. She had told him that she had met the Doctor but that she'd then lost him. Jack had told her not to worry and that he knew where the Doctor would be.

'He's gone to Downing Street to fight the Slitheen,' he had told her.

'How do you know?' she'd asked.

'Because it's what he does. And because he told me.'

'When?'

Jack had laughed. 'Oh, in my past but in his future. That's why I can't meet him. Isn't he amazing, though?'

'Yes. Yes, he is.'

As Toshiko watched the news, she wondered if that meant everything would be okay? Did that mean the Doctor would survive? Maybe, she thought, but what about the rest of us?

Mickey Smith and Jackie Tyler sat in Mickey's living room, towelling chunks of Slitheen out of their hair. They were safe and they had helped Rose – and the Doctor. Now all they had to do was wait. Mickey switched the television back on.

*

And in the Cabinet Office, the Doctor was brooding.

'What's wrong with him?' asked Harriet.

'He wants to be out there saving the world,' Rose replied. 'Instead, he's stuck in here and he hasn't got a clue what's going on.'

'But if we go outside, they'll kill us.'

The Doctor stood up. 'Why can't you be from just a couple of years into the future?' he asked Rose.

'Because it doesn't work like that?'

'In literally just a couple of years most of you apes will have smartphones. You'll have the internet, apps, videos, everything. Non-stop.'

'Oh,' said Harriet. 'I don't like the sound of that.'

'But if it was then, Harriet, we'd have the news on this.' He threw the phone down on the table. 'I'd know what was going on out there.'

'Yeah,' said Rose. 'But it's not then, it's now. So, wind your neck in and we'll sort something.'

Tom Hitchinson, standing outside 10 Downing Street reporting for BBC News, was shattered but determined to keep his place in the crowd. A well-built man had brought out a lectern suggesting that the acting Prime Minister might shortly be addressing the nation, and there was no way that Tom was going to miss that. He was the face of BBC

News today. For Tom Hitchinson, this had been a good day.

There was a sudden flurry of excitement. Tom turned to see the Prime Minister leave the building and take his place behind the lectern.

In his flat, Mickey quickly called Rose.

'Something's about to happen,' he said. He held his phone up against the television.

The crowd outside 10 Downing Street fell silent. The newsreaders in TV stations fell silent. The drinkers in the Green Dragon fell silent. The Doctor, Rose and Harriet Jones fell silent. The world fell silent.

Even Jackie Tyler fell silent.

The Prime Minister spoke.

'Ladies and gentlemen, nations of the world, humankind. The greatest experts in extraterrestrial events came here tonight. They gathered in the common cause, but the news I bring you now is grave indeed. The experts are dead, murdered right in front of me by alien hands. Peoples of the Earth, heed my words. These visitors do not come in peace. Our inspectors have searched the sky above our heads, and they have found massive weapons of destruction capable of being deployed within 45 seconds.

Our technicians can baffle the alien probes, but not for long. We are facing extinction unless we strike first. The United Kingdom stands directly beneath the belly of the mother ship. I beg of the United Nations, pass an emergency resolution. Give us the access codes. A nuclear strike at the heart of the beast is our only chance of survival – because from this moment on, it is my solemn duty to inform you, planet Earth is at war.'

14

Mutual Assured Destruction

The world, of course, descended into chaos.

The widespread looting of shops began almost immediately, especially in the United Kingdom, where most shops hadn't opened yet. Molly Steer watched through her window as youths trashed the newsagents and the chemist outside. She felt sad but she couldn't blame them. They'd just been told that their young lives were over before they had even begun. Those poor, poor kids. She went over to her wardrobe and took out the suit Denis had been wearing on their wedding day. Then she went and lay down on her bed, held the suit and imagined she was holding him.

Many families tried to leave London. Suitcases were packed and sleepy children were bundled onto back seats. The M1 out of London became one long traffic jam of unmoving cars and vans. A lot of people, mostly those without kids, stayed in their local pub. What would be would be, they figured. If these aliens could deploy their weapons in 45 seconds, then you had less than a minute to worry about your impending death. Meantime, get some in.

In Washington, America, President Arthur Winters immediately offered his assistance to any military operation against the invading aliens. He then shot a pistol into the air saying he was personally ready to bring down the alien scum. Moments later, when the cameras were switched off, he was scurrying to his car to be driven to the secret underground bunker where he'd be safe during any nuclear attack …

Under the Tower of London, Major Thomas Richard Blake at UNIT HQ realised that General Frost's team were among the dead at Downing Street, but he also knew that there was no time for grieving. He wondered where the Prime Minister had got his information from. Was it Torchwood? Was it even true?

'We will find out the truth,' he barked out to his team. 'For Muriel! Get to work!'

In Canary Wharf, Yvonne Hartman, the head of the London branch of the Torchwood Institute, instructed her workforce to start arming themselves with the alien technology they had acquired over the years. If there was going to be a war, then they were going to be ready.

Captain Jack Harkness, the head of the Welsh branch of the Torchwood Institute, sat in a shabby little café, holding a mug of coffee in his hands. He'd phoned each member of his team, telling them to be with their friends and lovers on this, the longest night. He knew, from what the Doctor had told him, that there was nothing they could do. He looked out, through the café window, at the dark skies above the city and he sipped his coffee. He just wished he wasn't alone.

In Trafalgar Square, people of all ages and all religions came together to sing. As the sky above them brightened with orange streaks of sunlight, they sang songs of hope. Many held hands.

In the courtyard of the Powell Estate, a young boy had found an old spray can and was spraying words onto the doors of the TARDIS. They were the words a beautiful glowing princess had whispered into his mind as he had slept. *Bad Wolf.*

And in New York, a small group of very important people gathered to decide whether to give the new Prime Minister of the United Kingdom the nuclear access codes ...

In the Cabinet Office, Rose watched the Doctor as he paced around the table. He wasn't used to being in one room for such a long period of time and he was clearly starting to struggle.

'He's making it up,' said the Doctor. 'There's no weapons up there, there's no threat. He just invented it.'

'Do you think they'll believe him?' asked Harriet.

Rose shrugged. 'They did last time.'

The Doctor strode over to the metal shutters keeping them safe. 'That's why the Slitheen went for spectacle. They want the whole world panicking, because you lot – you get scared, you lash out.'

'They release the defence codes,' said Rose, 'and the Slitheen go nuclear.'

'But why?' asked Harriet.

The Doctor hit the switch and the metal shutters opened. Three naked Slitheen and the one wearing Margaret Blaine's skin stood there, grinning at them.

The Doctor had worked it out. 'You get the codes, release the missiles, but not into space because there's nothing there. You attack every other country on Earth. They retaliate, fight back. World War Three. Whole planet gets nuked.'

The Margaret Blaine Slitheen giggled. 'And we can sit through it, safe in our spaceship waiting in the Thames. Not crashed, just parked. Only two minutes away.'

Harriet Jones was appalled. 'But you'll destroy the planet, this beautiful place. What for?'

'Profit,' sneered the Doctor. 'That's what the signal is beaming into space. An advert.'

'The sale of the century,' confirmed the Slitheen. 'We reduce the Earth to molten slag, then sell it piece by piece. Radioactive chunks, capable of powering every cut-price star liner and budget cargo ship. There's a recession out there, Doctor. People are buying cheap. This rock becomes raw fuel.'

The Doctor glared at her. 'At the cost of 6 billion lives.'

She shrugged. 'Bargain.'

The Doctor stepped outside of the Cabinet Room and pushed his face right into the face of the monster wearing Margaret Blaine's body. 'I give you a choice. Leave this planet or I'll stop you.'

'What, you?' she replied. 'Trapped in your box?'

'Yes,' he replied confidently, before stepping back into the room. 'Me.'

Rose had time to see just the tiniest flicker of fear on the Slitheen's face before the Doctor brought the metal shutters crashing down again.

The sun had risen over London and yet everything felt grey. Still standing outside the black door of 10

Downing Street, Tom Hitchinson looked into the camera. He thought about his father. Dad would be watching and he needed him to know that his son was definitely not scared.

'Yesterday saw the start of a brave new world. Today might see it end. Everyone's waiting, as the future is decided in New York.'

Trinity Wells was scared. For the first time in a very long time the news no longer felt like something she could use to get fame and fortune. She was remembering why she had become a journalist in the first place. To educate. To share the truth. Somehow, along the way, she had gotten caught up in all the glitz and the glamour.

Today, though, the news was truly terrifying, and she knew it was her job to share it accurately and calmly.

'It's midnight here in New York. The United Nations has gathered. England has provided them with absolute proof that the massive weapons of destruction do exist. The Security Council will be making a resolution in a matter of minutes and, if the codes are released, humanity's first interplanetary war begins.'

She gave her viewers a warm, genuine smile. 'Give your loved ones an extra hug tonight.'

As with pretty much everyone else on the planet, she didn't question the existence of the proof. It's usually just easier to believe what you are told.

PC Tristan White was sitting on the ground, in the carpark of the Green Dragon. He was drunk and he was crying. He tried to stop the tears as he reached into his pocket and took out his mobile phone. He dialled a number.

'Hi, Mum. Just thought I'd check in, see how you're doing ...'

Sergeant Donal Price stood to attention in the entrance hallway of 10 Downing Street. His men, some not much more than boys, lined each wall, ready to defend the most important building in the United Kingdom. He nodded to Joseph Green as he approached him. As ever, the Prime Minister was accompanied by General Asquith and Margaret Blaine. All three looked deadly serious.

'Sergeant.' The Prime Minister stopped in front of Donal. 'We'll take the call in the Prime Minister's office. Maintain your positions. Good luck.'

Green, Asquith and Blaine went up the stairs, and Sergeant Donal Price stood still. He thought about that girl in Hamburg. The one with the red hair who had asked him to dance in the town square fountain with her, so long ago.

He really wished he'd said yes.

As Sergeant Donal Price, PC Tristan White, Trinity Wells and everyone else on planet Earth considered what they'd done with their lives and what they'd do if there was any time left, Jocrassa Fel-Fotch Passameer-Day Slitheen, Styles Fel-Fotch Passameer-Day Slitheen and Blon Fel-Fotch Passameer-Day Slitheen entered the Prime Minister's office. They were laughing. They were thrilled to see the new addition on the Prime Minister's desk.

'Oh, look at that!' squealed Blon. 'The telephone is actually red!'

Jocrassa farted. 'How long until they phone?'

'Counting down,' said Styles, giggling.

Harriet Jones said goodbye to her mother and ended the call.

'Thank you for letting me borrow your phone,' she said to Rose, as she brushed away her tears. Her mother was fine. She didn't really understand what was going on, which was probably for the best. Harriet turned to the Doctor. 'If we could ferment the port, we could make acetic acid?'

The Doctor ignored her. He was clearly brooding about something.

Rose quickly called Mickey. They'd left him looking for numbers to call on the UNIT website.

'There's loads of emergency numbers,' his voice came through the speaker. 'They're all on voicemail.'

'Voicemail dooms us all,' muttered Harriet.

Rose was pacing the room now. Harriet wondered if she had any idea how much she and the Doctor subconsciously mimicked each other.

'If we could just get out of here,' said Rose.

The Doctor's voice was quiet. It was unnerving. 'There's a way out.'

Harriet and Rose both looked at him. 'What?!'

The Doctor was looking down at the floor. 'There's always been a way out.'

'Then why don't we use it?' asked Rose, clearly confused.

The Doctor slowly looked up. He walked over to the desk and spoke into the phone.

'Because I can't guarantee your daughter will be safe.'

Jackie's voice shrieked out from the speaker. 'Don't you dare. Whatever it is, don't you dare!'

'That's the thing. If I don't dare, *everyone* dies.'

Harriet stared at him.

Rose walked over to him and took his hand. 'Do it.'

He turned to face her. 'You don't even know what it is. You'd just let me?'

Rose nodded.

Harriet watched the Doctor and Rose as Jackie's sobbing voice sounded from the speaker.

'Doctor. Please. She's my daughter. She's just a kid.'

The Doctor looked so sad as he crouched down and whispered into the speaker. 'Do you think I don't know that? Because this is my life, Jackie. It's not fun, it's not smart, it's just standing up and making a decision because nobody else will.'

Rose put her hand on his shoulder. 'Then what're you waiting for?'

The Doctor looked up at her. 'I could save the world but lose you.'

Harriet knew that there was so little time. She knew that a decision needed to be made before 6 billion lives were snuffed out.

'Except it's not your decision, Doctor,' she said. 'It's mine.'

Jackie shrieked out. 'And who the hell are you?'

Harriet took a deep breath then took all the responsibility away from the Doctor. 'Harriet Jones, MP for Flydale North. The only elected representative in this room, chosen by the people for the people. And on behalf of the people, I command you. Do it.'

The Doctor looked up at her. There were tears in his eyes, and she wondered just how many painful decisions he had had to make in his life.

15

A Few Days Ago

Monday 7 March 2005, London
The Doctor glanced at Rose as they sat on a bench eating chips. He'd just shown her the end of her world, a sight nobody should witness. He'd thought she might be struggling to cope with what she'd seen and so, back in the TARDIS, he had set the coordinates for her time. He had brought her back to her world. He had brought her back home.

He had been scared, bringing her back to London, just in case it had all been too much for her and she wanted to leave him. But it hadn't been. She was eating chips, and she was grinning. Despite the events of the weekend, life was carrying on. So many had died, killed by the Nestene Consciousness. The Doctor looked around as workmen boarded up shop windows and the remains of shop dummies were swept away. He watched as the people of London wore brave determined smiles as they returned to work less than 48 hours after there'd been slaughter on the streets. Then he turned back to Rose. She was watching a giggling toddler chase after some clearly irritated pigeons. The toddler was clapping with delight as the pigeons scattered then regrouped around a discarded sandwich. The toddler jumped and giggled and the pigeons scattered and Rose Tyler laughed.

The Doctor had just told Rose about how his world was gone. Lost in battle. He had told her how he was the last of the Time Lords because there had been a war –

– the screaming, the confusion, the monsters, the shouting, the orders, the fire, so much fire –

He blinked. His hands were shaking. They always shook when he remembered.

– a soldier crying, a soldier dying, a soldier burning –

NO! London. Rose. Chips. Giggling toddler. Pigeons. He gripped the seat of the bench as he forced his hands to stop shaking and he tried not to remember –

– children, so many children on his world, missiles striking cities made of glass, fire, those monsters and –

He gripped the bench tighter, his knuckles so white. He wouldn't get lost in the nightmares, not any more. He had a friend now. He had Rose.

'I used to do that,' she said, pointing at the toddler. 'I wanted to take a pigeon home once. Keep it as a pet.' She laughed. 'Imagine my mum's face.'

The Doctor stared at anything, anything, anything – anything other than Rose. Because he hadn't told her everything.

– fire, fire, screaming children, fire, the monster, fire, the begging and pleading for it all to end and –

He had pressed the button. He had ended the War. His hands had ended the War.

And there had been silence. Had he done the right thing?

As the pigeons flew away and Rose Tyler offered him a handful of chips, the Doctor hoped he would never ever have to make a choice like that ever again.

16
BOOM!

Rose Tyler looked at the Doctor. 'How do we get out?'

'We don't. We stay here,' the Doctor replied. Then he spoke into the phone. 'Mickey, this is what I need you to do.'

Trinity Wells looked out at millions of viewers. 'The Council is voting. The results should be known any second now.'

Within seconds, the human race would know if they were at war.

In the Prime Minister's office, Blon Fel-Fotch Passameer-Day Slitheen stood up. She knew how the United Nations would vote. They had planned everything down to the last detail. She thought back to that first night when she'd chosen the pig to be their decoy astronaut. Such a simple thing. One little pig. And now this whole stupid, ugly rock and the billions who clung to it were about to be disintegrated.

'Victory should be naked!' her brother, Jocrassa declared and began to unzip his forehead.

Trinity Wells received the news she had been dreading.

'The vote is in. The Council says yes. They are releasing the codes.'

The world was going to war.

'What are you doing?' Jackie asked Mickey.

He turned to her and told her some of the Doctor's plan. 'Hacking into the Royal Navy.' He spoke into the phone. 'We're in. Here it is. HMS *Taurean*, Trafalgar Class submarine, ten miles off the coast of Plymouth.'

Jackie felt sick. She wanted to scream out, 'Why are you doing this?'

Why did it have to be Rose?

'Right, we need to select a missile,' the Doctor said to Mickey.

'We can't go nuclear. We don't have the defence codes.'

'We don't need it,' the Doctor replied. 'All we need's an ordinary missile. What's the first category?'

'Sub Harpoon, UGM-A4A.'

Rose held her breath waiting for the Doctor's response. Harriet just stared at him. He looked up at both of them.

'That's the one. Select.'

Rose and Harriet ran to join him. This was really happening.

Jackie stood up behind Mickey and looked down at him. 'I could stop you.'

Mickey looked up at her. He was as terrified as she was. He didn't even know why he was doing this. What life would he have if Rose died? But, somehow, he knew it was the right thing to do. 'Do it, then,' he replied.

Jackie just stared and Mickey could see in her eyes that she also knew it was the right thing to do. Rose might die but 6 billion people would live.

'You ready for this?' asked the Doctor.

Mickey's voice was barely a whisper. 'Yeah.'

In the Cabinet Room, the Doctor looked down at the telephone.

'Mickey the Idiot. The world is in your hands.'

*

Jocrassa Fel-Fotch Passameer-Day Slitheen was staring at the red telephone.

'Ring, damn you!'

He looked up as the rest of his beautiful naked family entered the room and joined them.

'Welcome, my brothers and sisters. Welcome to the biggest payday of our lives.'

Mickey stared at the website in front of him and waited for the command.

The Doctor read out a series of coordinates. Mickey repeated them as he typed them.

'But where are they for?' asked Jackie. 'Where are you attacking?'

'Fire,' said the Doctor, simply and calmly.

'Tell me,' Jackie wailed.

Mickey Smith calmly pressed the big red button marked 'fire' and activated a missile. A rocket launched from the HMS *Taurean* submarine.

Its destination was Downing Street.

Rose watched as Harriet Jones started hitting the metal shutters.

'How solid are these?' she asked.

The Doctor looked guilty. 'Not solid enough. Built for short-range attack, nothing this big.'

Rose wanted to slap him. They were not giving in. 'All right, now I'm making the decision. I'm not going to die. We're going to ride this one out. It's like what they say about earthquakes. You can survive them by standing under a doorframe.' She ran over to one of the cupboards that were built into the wall. 'Now, this cupboard's small so it's strong. Come and help me. Come on.'

She started emptying the cupboard. Harriet and the Doctor ran over and joined her.

There was always hope.

Mickey stared at his computer. It took him a minute to work out what he was looking at. UNIT were fighting back: missiles were being sent to shoot their stolen missile down. But Mickey Smith had spent the previous year hacking into websites, desperate to find out anything he could about the Doctor.

And what Mickey Smith realised, as he started to neutralise UNIT's counter-attack, was that the Doctor wasn't always right. Because Mickey Smith was no idiot.

'Counter-defence five-five-six.'

'Stop them intercepting it,' ordered the Doctor.

'I'm doing it now!' Mickey replied as his fingers danced across the keyboard. 'Five-five-six neutralised. Easy,' he said with a grin. Then remembering Jackie, he turned to look at her.

'They'll be okay,' he said. 'They will.'

Jackie was just staring at the opposite wall. She looked broken.

Sergeant Donal Price was still standing in the entrance hallway of 10 Downing Street. Constable Neil Murphy suddenly came running towards him.

'Sir, there's a missile incoming.'

'What do you mean incoming?'

'It's heading towards London. Central London.' Neil Murphy pointed up. 'It's heading towards us.'

Sergeant Donal Price considered his orders. He and his team had been ordered to maintain their positions. Orders were orders until they heard otherwise.

He stared at Constable Murphy. He stared at the man who would die if he continued to unthinkingly obey the rules. Then he walked over to the nearest wall and slammed his hand down on the fire alarm manual call point.

'Get out!' he yelled.

The missile reached the British Isles. It flew across the white cliffs of Dover and headed, with deadly precision, towards its target.

It couldn't be stopped now.

Donal ran out onto Downing Street, to the waiting journalists and TV crews.

'Get away from here, now. We're under attack!'

Tom Hitchinson frowned. 'Attack?'

'There's a bloody great big missile heading straight for us! Run!'

Donal ran back into the building and straight through until he reached the back entrance. The final ambulance crews were ready to leave with the bodies of the murdered experts.

'Drive! Drive! Drive!' he yelled at them, and they started to drive away.

Donal ran back inside. The last few civil servants were running out through the front door. Donal saw one official struggling to carry a computer out with him. He ran over, grabbed the computer out of his hands, threw it down and shoved the man out through the door. 'Nothing is more important than your life, you idiot!'

He turned back and saw Constable Murphy. 'Is that everyone?'

Murphy nodded.

'And all our lads?'

Murphy nodded.

'I can still see one standing in front of me,' said Donal, putting a hand on Neil's shoulder.

'What about you, sir?'

'There's been no sign of the Prime Minister or his pals. Someone needs to tell them. Leave now, Murphy, that's an order.'

Donal could tell Neil was going to argue so he raised his gun. 'It's an order, Neil. Get out. My duty is to protect the Prime Minister.'

Constable Neil Murphy grabbed Donal's hand and shook it. Then he ran.

The missile flew over South London. Jackie Tyler ran out and watched it fly over the Powell Estate. She stared at it, barely able to comprehend what she was seeing. A missile flying through the Estate. She thought about all the wars she'd seen on the telly. The missiles in Iraq. She'd never believed it could happen here.

Then she heard a horrific heartbreaking noise and she turned to see Mickey sobbing.

'What have I done?' he asked her. She ran over and held him as he wept.

Tristan ended the call with his mum and looked up as the missile flew over the Green Dragon. Andi and Emma joined him and they looked up at the sky. At least they had each other. They sat there in their police uniforms, as helpless as everyone else.

Donal began to climb the stairs. He was, by now, convinced that Joseph Green was behind whatever was happening tonight. But he wasn't a judge or a jury. It wasn't his place to decide who got to live and who got to die. As he climbed the stairs, he could hear the missile's whistling high above as it started its descent. He ran up the stairs and towards the Prime Minister's office.

In the Cabinet Office, Rose Tyler, the Doctor and Harriet Jones, MP for Flydale North, crouched down into the back of the cupboard. All three looked up at the terrifying sound of the approaching missile.

Donal didn't bother to knock on the door to the Prime Minister's office. He barged in.

'Sir, there's a missile—'

He stopped. He looked at the group of tall green aliens just standing there as if tall green aliens just standing anywhere was a normal thing.

'Sorry,' he muttered, as he turned and ran.

*

The Doctor took Rose's hand, and then he took Harriet's hand.

Harriet gave them both a warm smile. 'Here we go. Nice knowing you both.' Then, as the three of them clutched each other and they heard the horrific sound of the deadly missile crashing through the roof three floors above them, Harriet Jones, MP for Flydale North, suddenly yelled out a single word: 'Hannibal!'

The Slitheen had all looked up as the strange whistling sound above them became an ear-shattering scream, and as something came crashing through the roof, one floor above them. So they were all looking up at the ceiling when for the briefest of seconds there was no ceiling, just a missile hurtling down towards them. Every member of the Slitheen family instantly realised that they weren't going to be rich and that perhaps they'd underestimated the human race.

Blon just blinked. 'Oh, bol—'

The missile tore through every floor of 10 Downing Street and exploded. The famous building was instantly transformed into a ball of fire. Bricks. Windows. The iconic black door. Everything was destroyed.

17

Should I Stay or Should I Go?

Everything was dark for Sergeant Donal Price. He presumed this was death. He'd died, as he had lived, as a good obedient soldier. Except he hadn't, he thought to himself. He'd disobeyed his orders and he'd saved people. Then he realised that with all this thinking he was probably still alive. He opened his eyes and saw the devastated remains of Downing Street. He staggered to his feet and looked out across the rubble.

That was the moment he decided to retire.

As the smoke started to clear, Donal saw a large metal box. He started to move towards it when, suddenly, a door in the box opened. Three people staggered out. He ran over to them.

'Made in Britain,' the older woman was saying.

Donal took her hand and helped her down. 'Are you all right?'

She nodded. 'Harriet Jones. MP, Flydale North. I want you to contact the UN immediately. Tell the ambassadors the crisis is over. They can stand down. Go on, tell the news.'

'Yes, ma'am.' Donal headed off.

He would do this one last task and then he would hand in his notice.

Nobody would ever know how many lives Donal Price had saved that day. And that was just how he wanted it.

Mickey and Jackie were watching the news. Tom Hitchinson had decided to return to get as close to the remains of 10 Downing Street as he could. Mickey and Jackie watched silently as the smoke started to clear.

Then they saw them. The Doctor and Rose, climbing down over the rubble with Harriet Jones. Rose, seeing the BBC camera, turned and looked directly at them. She gave them a wave.

Jackie pulled Mickey into a hug and didn't let go.

Rose stared back at what remained of 10 Downing Street.

'My boyfriend did that,' she said, smiling.

Harriet nodded. 'Someone's got a hell of a job sorting this lot out. Oh, Lord. We haven't even got a Prime Minister.'

The Doctor grinned at her. 'Maybe you should have a go.'

Harriet shook her head. 'Me? Huh. I'm only a backbencher.'

'I'd vote for you,' said Rose as the three of them started to walk back onto Parliament Road.

'Now, don't be silly,' Harriet replied. 'Look, I'd better go and see if I can help. Hang on!'

As Harriet headed off towards some waiting police officers, she called out, 'We're safe! The Earth is safe!'

The Doctor suddenly turned to Rose. 'I thought I knew the name. Harriet Jones, future Prime Minister. Elected for three successive terms. The architect of Britain's Golden Age!'

Rose grinned back at him. A Golden Age sounded good!

Rose linked her arm with his and they started to head home.

'What does he eat?'

Rose looked over at her mum. 'How do you mean?'

'I was going to do shepherd's pie. All of us. A proper sit down, cos I'm ready to listen,' Jackie said. 'I wanna learn about you and him and that life you lead. Only, I don't know, he's an alien. For all I know, he eats grass and safety pins and things.'

Rose laughed. 'He'll have shepherd's pie. You're going to cook for him?'

'What's wrong with that?'

'He's finally met his match.'

Her mum laughed. 'You're not too old for a slap, you know.' She got up and went through to the kitchen.

Rose turned back to watch the TV when her phone started ringing. She looked down at it and smiled. A cute little blue police box had appeared on the screen. The caller ID was 'TARDIS'.

'Hello?'

It was the Doctor, of course. 'Right, I'll be a couple of hours, then we can go.'

'You've got a phone?'

'You think I can travel through time and space, and I haven't got a phone? Like I said, couple of hours.'

Rose grimaced. 'My mother's cooking.'

'Good,' replied the Doctor. 'Put her on a low heat and let her simmer.'

Rose laughed. 'She's cooking tea. For us.'

The Doctor's voice was flat. 'I don't do that.'

'It's just tea.'

'Not to me it isn't.'

'She's my mother!'

'Well, she's not mine.'

Again, Rose wondered just why he was so determined not to get close to others.

'Well, you can stay there if you want,' he said. 'But right now there's this plasma storm brewing in the Horsehead Nebula. Fires are burning 10 million miles wide. I could fly the TARDIS right into the heart of it then ride the shock wave all the way out. Hurtle right across the sky and end up anywhere. Your choice.'

He ended the call.

Mickey Smith was sitting on a bin in the courtyard of the Powell Estate. He was staring at a fox as the fox, standing totally still, stared right back at him.

'What?' he said to the fox. 'What are you looking at?'

There was something about the fox that made Mickey feel sad. It was solitary. Alone. No friends. No family. Just the fox. Just a poor dumb animal looking for food and maybe a friend.

Just like me, thought Mickey

As the fox turned and trotted away, Mickey watched the Doctor step out of the TARDIS. A young boy had just finished scrubbing graffiti off the police box doors. The Doctor spoke to him briefly then the boy headed off.

The Doctor gave Mickey a small wave and headed over to join him. They hadn't seen each other since before they'd blown up Downing Street together. 'That boy,' said the Doctor. 'He had the strangest dream.'

Mickey, though, had no time for small talk. 'I just went down the shop, and I was thinking, you know, like the whole world's changed. Aliens and spaceships all in public. And here it is.' He held up a newspaper. The headline read 'ALIEN HOAX'.

'They're just not ready,' replied the Doctor. 'You're happy to believe in something that's invisible, but if it's staring you in the face, nope, can't see it. There's a scientific explanation for that: you're thick.'

Mickey looked at him. 'We're just idiots.'

There was a pause then the Doctor gave him a small smile. 'Well, not all of you.'

There was something about the Doctor's smile, that hint of respect, that made Mickey feel as if, maybe, just maybe, he would be all right.

The Doctor handed him a CD. 'That's a virus. Put it online. It'll destroy every mention of me. I'll cease to exist.'

'What do you want to do that for?'

'Because you're right, I am dangerous. I don't want anybody following me.'

Mickey looked over at the door leading to the stairwell. Rose was pushing through the door, Jackie following.

'How can you say that,' he asked, 'and then take her with you?'

'You could look after her,' the Doctor replied. He took a deep breath and then he said it. 'Come with us.'

Mickey felt the Earth shift. He imagined seeing what they saw. He imagined fighting the monsters. Then he remembered sitting in the garage clenching his fists, trying not to cry. He remembered sobbing after seeing the missile heading towards Downing Street.

Mickey Smith had lost his mother and then his grandmother. His father had left him. He'd been through so much but he'd never really talked about it to anyone. He'd always tried not to think about it. He was starting to realise now, though, that maybe he should talk to someone about what he'd been through. Maybe he needed help or maybe he was fine. He just wasn't sure.

'I can't,' he replied. 'This life of yours, it's just too much. I couldn't do it. Don't tell her I said that.'

The Doctor looked at him then briefly took his hand. He smiled at Mickey, a smile that seemed to say that everything would be okay. Then he let go of his hand and they turned to look at Jackie and Rose.

An hour ago, Jackie Tyler had found her daughter in her bedroom, packing her rucksack. Silently, she'd gone back into the kitchen and turned off the oven. She remembered that long night a year before, sitting in the dark, waiting for Rose to come home. And now, it was happening again.

She looked over at the fridge. One of the magnets on the door of the fridge was a photo of her Pete, her ridiculous, beautiful, annoying, funny, handsome Pete, grinning out at her every day. She went over and took the magnet off the fridge door. She could go through to Rose and she could beg her not to leave her. She could remind her how Pete was gone and how if she left then she'd –

Jackie put the photo down. That would be wrong. She would try and persuade Rose to stay, but not like that.

Mickey watched as Jackie chased after Rose. 'I'll get a proper job. I'll work weekends. I'll pass my test, and if Jim comes round again, I'll say no. I really will.'

'I'm not leaving because of you. I'm travelling, that's all, and then I'll come back.'

Mickey noticed that Rose had packed a rucksack. A big rucksack.

Jackie had tears in her eyes. 'But it's not safe.'

'Mum, if you saw it out there, you'd never stay home.'

'Got enough stuff?' the Doctor asked, spotting the rucksack.

'Last time I stepped in there, it was spur of the moment. Now I'm signing up. You're stuck with me.'

Laughing, she flung the rucksack at the Doctor then she turned to Mickey. 'Come with us, there's plenty of room.'

Before Mickey could speak, the Doctor answered. 'No chance. He's a liability, I'm not having him on board.'

'We'd be dead without him,' Rose said, turning to face the Doctor.

'My decision is final.'

Mickey gave the Doctor a tiny nod of gratitude. Rose turned back to her boyfriend and kissed him on the cheek.

Jackie turned to face the Doctor. 'You still can't promise me. What if she gets lost? What if something happens to you, Doctor, and she's left all alone standing on some moon a million light years away? How long do I wait then?'

'Mum, you're forgetting. It's a time machine.' Rose hugged her mum. 'I could go travelling around suns and planets and all the way out to the edge of the universe, and by the time I get back, yeah, ten seconds would have passed. Just ten seconds. So, stop worrying. See you in ten seconds' time, yeah?'

Rose let go of Jackie and, without looking back, she followed the Doctor into the TARDIS.

Jackie and Mickey watched as the blue box faded out of existence.

They waited.

Five seconds. Ten seconds.

Jackie smiled sadly at Mickey then turned to head back towards the stairwell. That was it, then. She was alone again. No Pete, no Rose. But then she looked up at the flats in front of her and she smiled properly. She wasn't alone, not really. She had a friend in every single one of those lit-up windows. Tomorrow, she thought, I'll check in on Molly, and I'll see if Ru wants to go to the bingo and –

She stopped and turned back. Mickey Smith was just standing there. He hadn't moved.

Jackie realised that she might not really be alone, but he was. She called over to him. 'I've made a shepherd's pie. If you want some.'

The boy, because he was still just a boy, nodded and walked over to join her. She held out her hand and he took it. They heard laughter coming from one of the flats. It was Molly Steer. They looked over and could see into her kitchen. Inside, Molly was laughing and dancing with two young policemen and a policewoman. All four celebrating life.

'We'll be fine,' Jackie said to Mickey. He nodded and smiled. 'Oh, but when I say I made a shepherd's pie ...'

Mickey Smith laughed. 'Frozen ready meal?'

'Yeah.' Jackie Tyler giggled. 'But I'll sprinkle some cheddar on it. Proper fancy.'

Holding hands, the two friends headed home.

18

Meanwhile, 4.9 miles away from the Powell Estate . . .

Captain Jack Harkness has left the café and now he stands in the shadows. His phone rings and he quickly answers it, his voice a whisper.

'Yes, Tosh?'

'Is it over?' she asks. 'Really? Is it all over?'

He forces himself to smile. 'You bet. The Doctor's saved us all. Now go to sleep. Tomorrow's a bright new day.'

'Goodnight, Jack.'

'Night.'

He ends the call.

He knows he shouldn't be here. He shouldn't be in London, but that morning he'd followed Tosh to the heliport and taken the next flight. Staying in the shadows, avoiding public transport, the soldiers on the streets and anyone who might know him, he had made his way across London to here, to the Isle of Dogs. He looks up again at One Canada Square, at the tower that dominates the skyline. Lights shining out into the night sky, like a beacon calling out to alien life. In one of the building's windows he can see a young man, handsome, dressed in a suit, staring out at the world.

Then Jack looks back over at the large industrial bin across the street. It's dark and still now but he saw the bright green light that briefly erupted from inside it at the exact moment the missile had struck 10 Downing Street.

He's been standing there ever since, waiting and watching.

The silence of the street is suddenly disturbed by a low groan coming from inside the bin. The bin shifts slightly as something inside it starts to move. Jack watches as the lid of the bin slowly starts to rise, pushed open from the inside by a hand that looks human but isn't. He watches as the creature that transported itself into the bin at the exact moment the missile struck 10 Downing Street stands to its full height. It is, as he knew it would be, still wearing the skinsuit of Margaret Blaine.

Jack watches as the Slitheen climbs out of the bin and brushes rubbish and debris from its skinsuit. It would be so easy for him to kill it now. But he knows that to do so would change his own history.

And so he only watches as the very ordinary-looking Margaret Blaine walks off into the night, into her future and into Jack Harkness's past.

Epilogue

'Where are we going?' asked Rose as the TARDIS hurtled through the Time Vortex.

'You'll see,' said the Doctor.

Rose felt the TARDIS stop and everything become still. Without asking, she rushed to the doors and opened them. She looked out ... 'You have got to be joking.'

It was a shed. A huge shed, dark and stinking, with what seemed to be hundreds of pigs crammed in with barely any room to move or breathe. Rose had never seen so many creatures looking so broken and without hope. It was horrific. The Doctor joined her at the door.

'Clyne Mount farm,' he said. 'The pig – the one the Slitheen tortured, used, defiled – he came from here. Now, stand back.'

Rose stood back and the Doctor oinked. Loudly. With a northern accent. Every single pig in the barn slowly turned to look at him. The Doctor oinked again, and the pigs started to shuffle towards the TARDIS.

'Stand back,' said the Doctor. 'Pigs incoming!'

Rose backed herself into the wall as hundreds of pigs started to push their way into the TARDIS.

Minutes but also centuries later, on an alien planet, where the sky was turquoise and the water smelled of rosemary, the TARDIS materialised. The doors opened and the Doctor and Rose ushered the pigs out. Hundreds of pigs, some big, some small, headed out into the biggest meadow ever. Some, for the first time in their lives, were running.

'This planet, it's unique,' said the Doctor, folding his arms and leaning against the TARDIS. 'It never gets discovered by humans or any other species. It remains untouched until the end of the universe. I couldn't save Barry, but I can do this.'

Rose turned to look at the Doctor. 'You are fantastic. Hang on – "Barry"?!'

They grinned at each other, waved at the happy pigs then stepped back into the TARDIS. The light on top of the TARDIS started to glow and flash, the wheezing and groaning sound echoing across the planet.

And then there was no sound at all, save for contented oinks and the munching of grass.

Acknowledgements

I've written a *Doctor Who* Target novelisation! Mind actually blown!

Many, many, many thanks to my reading crew of Dónal Borg-Neal, Rob Morris, Emma Reeves and Tristan Fear.

As always, with every job I'll ever have, much love to James Goss and Gary Russell for giving me such amazing opportunities all those years ago.

Thanks to Albert DePetrillo for giving me this opportunity and to Steve Cole for being such an amazing, supportive and understanding editor.

Thanks to Mum, Dad, Jen, James and all their various offspring for being the best family.

And this novelisation is a love letter to everyone involved in the production of the 2005 series of *Doctor Who*. You changed television, you brilliant, brilliant people xx